Fire at the Track

A Harness Racing Mystery

Fire

at the

Track

A Harness Racing Mystery

M.J. Evans

Dancing Horse Press

M.J. Evans/Dancing Horse Press
7013 S. Telluride St.
Foxfield, CO 80016
www.dancinghorsepress.com

Publisher's Note: This is a work of fiction. Names, characters, places, and incidents are a product of the author's imagination. Locales and public names are sometimes used for atmospheric purposes. Any resemblance to actual people, living or dead, or to businesses, companies, events, institutions, or locales is completely coincidental.

Publisher's Cataloging-in-Publication Data: Name: M.J. Evans, Author. Dancing Horse Press (2026) Foxfield, CO. Age Level: 18 and up. Summary: Insurance investigator Callie Oaks goes undercover at Liberty Racetrack to find who killed twenty-eight horses in a suspicious fire. When the arsonist discovers her identity and tries to kill her, Callie must expose the truth before she becomes the next victim.

Library of Congress Control Number: 2026900732

Fire at the Track / M.J. Evans. - 1st ed.
ISBN 979-8-9938794-0-6

Author's Note

On July 6, 2001, a fire at the Meadows Harness Racing Track in Washington, Pennsylvania, claimed the lives of twenty-eight horses. The cause was never determined. On November 7, 2023, another barn fire at Tioga Downs in New York killed thirty horses and a cat; a man was later convicted of arson, though his motive remains unknown.

These tragic events inspired *Fire at the Track*, but this is a work of fiction. The characters, investigation, and resolution are entirely products of my imagination. While I've used the Meadows incident as a backdrop for realism, the story you're about to read is not based on fact, and any resemblance to real people or events is coincidental.

I acknowledge these real tragedies with deep sorrow for the horses lost and offer this story in their memory.

Contents

Above the din of the crowd, the announcer's voice cut through the afternoon air, sharp and electric. "Nine of our finest three-year-old Standardbred pacers are vying today to qualify for harness racing's Pacing Triple Crown."

Tommy Valdez shifted in his box seat, fingers drumming against his knee. The harness racing Triple Crown. Three races that separate legends from also-rans: The Messenger Stakes in Yonkers, New York; The Cane Pace, which is held at Meadowlands Racetrack in East Rutherford, New Jersey, and finishing at the Little Brown Jug at the Delaware County Fair in Delaware, Ohio.

The announcer continued, his enthusiasm building.

"The Little Brown Jug being the third leg of the Pacing Triple Crown is always held on the third Thursday after Labor Day, so pacing fans, you won't want to miss it."

A roar went up from the grandstand as the horses passed, their muscled bodies gleaming in the sun. The drivers, in their colorful jumpsuits and helmets, acknowledged the crowd with waves. Tommy rose halfway from his seat, heart pounding.

"Ladies and Gentlemen, keep your eyes on the two horse, the big bay. He's today's favorite—Eat My Dust, owned by local breeder Tommy Valdez."

Tommy barely heard the cheer that followed his name. His attention locked on the track, on the massive bay colt pacing behind the mobile starting gate's metal arms. Stanley Smithfield, purple and gold suit vivid against the limestone track, sat low in the sulky, hands steady on the lines.

Second position. Perfect.

The starting gate rolled forward, picking up speed. The horses fell into formation behind it, their lateral gait building momentum. Eat My Dust moved like liquid metal, smooth and powerful. Tommy's chest tightened.

"And they're off," shouted the announcer into his microphone as the long arms of the starting gate swung forward and the starting car to which they were attached sped off. The nine pacers, now free to begin racing, burst forward in their distinctive wobbly, two-sided, lateral gait. Right front and right back moving forward together, followed by left front and left back. Repeat, repeat, repeat, faster and faster. The thunder of hooves against the limestone surface of the track rolled past the grandstand. Nine drivers, leaning back in their sulkies, jockeyed for the best spot as the announcer called out the drama unfolding before the throng of harness racing fans.

"Eat My Dust is living up to his name!" The

announcer's voice climbed an octave. "He is pacing strongly and has already crossed over against the pylons well before the opening turn!"

Purple and gold flashed against the inside pylons. Eat My Dust hugged the rail, putting distance between himself and the field. Tommy watched the infield clock: 26.4 seconds at the quarter pole. Tommy's pulse hammered in his ears. *Not too fast. Don't burn out.*

54.4 seconds at the half.

Tommy Valdez was on his feet now, fist pumping the air. Around him, the crowd roared, but he heard nothing except the blood rushing through his head and the rhythmic cadence of his horse's hooves.

By the three-quarter mark, Eat My Dust opened up a four-length lead. The other horses pushed hard, drivers urging them forward, but the big bay was untouchable. He stretched his lead, eating up ground with every powerful stride.

Horse and driver streaked past the finish line as the infield clock flashed 1:48.3.

"And that, ladies and gentlemen, is a new track record!"

The grandstand exploded. Tommy stood frozen in his box, staring at the clock, at his horse coming down to a slow jog, at Smithfield raising one hand in triumph as he guided the bay around the turn. The noise washed over him—cheers, applause, the announcer's continued commentary—but Tommy felt suspended in a single perfect moment.

A track record.

His horse. His breeding program. His gamble.

Then reality crashed back. The syndication deal was taking shape. Maybe this would convince the prospective investors to go forward.

Everything depended on what happened next.

Chapter 2

ASHVILLE GAZETTE-SPORTS

EAT MY DUST SHATTERS TRACK RECORD AT LIBERTY
By Paul Coffman

ASHVILLE, PA – Local breeder Tommy Valdez's three-year-old Standardbred pacer Eat My Dust lived up to his name Saturday, setting a new track record of 1:48.3 at Liberty Racetrack.

The bay stallion, driven by Stanley Smithfield, dominated the field from start to finish...

Paul Coffman, sports reporter for the local paper, bent over his keyboard, trying to beat his deadline.

As he created an article for the next day's edition of the Ashville Gazette, his editor leaned over his shoulder.

"Good piece on the Valdez horse, Coffman. But I need more than race results. Find me a story with teeth."

That night, Barn 7 was the scene of a joyous celebration. All the owners, trainers, and drivers who had been assigned to that barn by the racetrack's paddock judge had become a sort of family. One's success was everyone's success. And in a way, one's failure was everyone's failure.

On this occasion there was much to celebrate with Eat My Dust's stunning record-setting victory. Everyone in the barn affectionately called the three-year-old colt "Dusty," and they were all thrilled that he had qualified to compete in this year's Pacing Triple Crown, the three races that made up harness racing's prestigious championship.

Up to thirty horses at a time were stabled in Barn 7. Some owners had four horses housed there. Some had only two or three in the barn yet owned several more horses not yet competing that they kept at their farms. Others, such as Marcus Brennan, were putting all their eggs in one stall, so to speak, owning only one horse. Brennan's horse, Thunder's Echo, was stabled in the end stall in Barn 7.

Tommy Valdez, a short man with jet black hair and a trimmed goatee, was enjoying the spotlight as he toasted his horse and made speeches about his plans for the future. Dusty would be prepared and ready to shine at The Cane Pace, still a few weeks away. In the meantime, his trainer and driver would be working with him regularly and entering him in a few more races at the Liberty track just to keep him on top of his game.

Paul Coffman, reporter for the local paper, the *Ashville Gazette*, asked, "When will he race next?"

Valdez grinned. "I have him set to race again just a week from now, on July 7th."

Suddenly, Coffman's questioning took a surprising turn. "Any truth to the rumor that some of the horses have been found with D-Methamphetamine in their systems?"

A hush fell over the group of friends. All eyes turned to Valdez. The boisterous owner puffed up his chest, "Certainly not *my* horses." His face twisted in disgust. "You can check the records from the track veterinarian, Dr. Paige Taylor. She keeps a close eye on all the horses in Barn 7. She even confided in me that she'll be doing blood tests the day before the next race day."

Murmurings floated through the crowd as Coffman continued his questioning. "What about the horses in the other barns? Might they be using drugs?"

"I can't speak for them. I would certainly hope not. We don't want any black marks on our sport." Valdez turned his attention to an attractive middle-aged woman who threw her arms around his chest and kissed him on the cheek as Coffman drifted away.

Sarah Ferguson, her smooth complexion and petite frame belying her fifty years, was the owner of several mares as part of her breeding operation. She had been in the harness racing world longer than anyone could remember. At the moment, two of her mares were being raced and part of the Barn 7 family.

"Oh, Tommy! I can't tell you how happy I am for you. I watched the race. Dusty was simply marvelous. And your new driver, what's his name? Stanley?"

"Stanley Smithfield." His face beamed.

"Yes. He knew just what he was doing."

"I'm very pleased to have him on the team. He's training and driving several of my horses."

"Well, aren't you the lucky one." Ferguson flipped a strand of curly, bleached blond hair out of her eyes.

"*You* seem to be doing well with your mares all of a sudden." Valdez cocked his head.

"I have a new man training, and driving them, as well. He really seems to have a knack for working with mares. Not everyone does, as you know."

"Yes. Mares can be quite persnickety." A knowing twinkle was noticeable in his eye.

"Tell me about it." She lowered her voice. "What is this about drug testing?"

Valdez lowered his voice. "Dr. Taylor is going to draw blood on every horse in our barn before the next weekend's races. I know she won't find anything in Barn 7."

"Certainly not. Not in our horses." Ferguson gave Valdez another peck on the cheek. "I couldn't be happier for you and sweet Dusty." Turning on her heel, she moved over to the refreshment table to fill a plate with the hors d'oeuvres Valdez had catered for the celebration.

As soon as she left, Joey Castellano grabbed Valdez's upper arm and pulled the horse owner into an empty stall. Nicknamed "Numbers," Castellano was the local backstretch bookie who worked the harness racing track full time. While the pari-mutuel betting was going on in the clubhouse, Numbers had his own business going under-the-table, so to speak.

His stocky but muscular frame gave him the ability to push people around if he wanted to. And he often wanted to. Most people were intimidated by Castellano and tended to avoid him.

"What are you doing here, Castellano?" Valdez sneered, his eyes searching the crowd to see if anyone noticed their interaction. He jerked his arm away from the bookie's hold. "This is a private party."

It had taken years of practice, but now Castellano could respond to any affront calmly, or so he liked to think, *professionally*. "Forgive me for being a party crasher." Castellano's voice dripped with mock sincerity. "I merely wanted to congratulate you on your victory today. I'll let you go back to the celebration. I'm sure I'll be hearing from you soon, will I not?"

Castellano chuckled and left Valdez alone in the dark stall. Valdez felt a trickle of sweat roll down the side of his face.

"Tommy, my man. Where are you?"

Valdez stepped out of the stall to find an old friend calling for him. "Right here, Curtis."

"Hey! There's the man of the hour." Curtis Meier slapped Valdez on the back. The man was a wealthy entrepreneur, well-liked by everyone in Ashville. "Couldn't be happier for you. Show me that famous horse of yours."

As the two men stood in front of Dusty's stall, an idea crystallized in Valdez's mind. An idea he'd been toying with for a while. An idea that would solve his problems. "Say, Curtis, I've been thinking about selling shares in Dusty—syndicating him to spread the wealth among my friends, you know. Interested?"

"Am I interested? You bet I am! I know lots of other people who would be, too. Let's have coffee next week and discuss the details."

The sun had long since set. The evening feedings were complete. The horses were bedded down for the night and most of the Barn 7 family had returned to their homes after cleaning up the party goods.

One stall at the very end of the east side of the aisle remained lit. The stall was leased to Marcus Brennan, a computer technician who had recently quit his corporate job and was working on his own as a consultant. This enabled him to spend more time with the love of his life, his stallion, Thunder's Echo.

The chestnut had good bone and a steady eye, which was more than most people could say for Brennan's chances. Green as spring grass in the harness game, he'd bought himself four legs of trouble and called it his future. But it proved to be a matter of pure luck that Thunder, in his second year of racing, had racked up quite a few wins and had a promising future. He was already valued at $250,000, and Brennan had reason to hope for more wins followed by a successful career as a stud. If Thunder's Echo worked out, Brennan dreamt of adding more horses to his stable.

He was kneeling in the straw bedding, putting leg wraps around Thunder's legs when the quiet of the barn was interrupted as the stall door jerked open with a bang. Startled, he pivoted and saw his wife, jaw set, eyes narrowed, standing in the opening. Thunder let out a threatening snort and pinned his ears.

"Marcus, I'm not going to put up with this anymore." A tear rolled down her cheek. "I can't compete with this horse addiction you've developed."

Marcus stood and stepped toward her, his arms extended. "Oh, Dianne, don't be like this. I'm only doing this for us. This horse is going to make us rich."

"Rich?" she screeched. She rummaged through her purse and pulled out a piece of paper, shaking it in front of his face. "Rich, you say? This horse is putting us in the poor house. It's bad enough that you quit your job, a great job with a steady income, but look how much this horse is costing us! Look! I've printed out just two months of expenses. Need I enumerate them for you? Board, feed, shoeing, vet bills, entrance fees, a new sulky, harness repairs…it goes on and on with no end in sight."

"He's bringing in money with his wins. And that's just the beginning. Wait until the stud fees start rolling in."

"And that will be…?"

"In just a couple of years."

"And then what? Then you buy more horses?"

"Well, yes. That *is* the plan."

She wadded up the paper and threw it to the ground. "This is not a plan that I signed on to when we got married. You never said anything about horses," she said, brushing the tears from her cheeks. "I want a husband who does things with *me*. I want a family, children, and a husband who takes care of us. We've been married for over five years. But instead of my dreams coming true, I have no children and no husband—you're always here with that…that…four-legged beast!"

Thunder snorted again, tossing his head and stomping a front hoof.

Feeling defensive on Thunder's behalf, Marcus did his best to control his temper. He didn't want to scare the horse, after all. "Don't be mad at Thunder. He's not to blame for *my* behavior." He rubbed the stallion's neck.

Stepping up to Dianne, he put his hands on her shoulders and, working to keep his voice calm for the horse's sake: "I know you are suffering from losing your pregnancy. I am, too."

Dianne jerked away. "It doesn't seem like it."

Marcus dropped his gaze and shoved his hands in his pockets. "I know you didn't sign up for this. I understand that. I had no idea I'd be doing this myself. But Thunder fills a void in my life that I can't really explain. I wish I could make you understand how important Thunder is to me. How much I love this whole world," he said, making a sweeping motion with his chin.

"A world that doesn't include me." Her jaw clenched.

"But it can." He looked up, his eyes pleading, his hands coming out of his pockets and reaching toward her. "It can if only you would let it. There are lots of husband-and-wife teams in harness racing. They do it together. *We* could do it together."

Dianne stepped back and Marcus dropped his hands to his side. "You're not listening to me." Anger rose in her voice. "I don't want to be a part of this *world* as you call it. I want children—not a big fur baby as this generation wants to call their animals."

She started to run toward the barn door, stopped, turned, and shouted back at Marcus who still stood in the stall's doorway. "Don't come home. I'll have your things sent to Thunder's stall."

"Dianne, don't do this."

But Dianne was not there to hear it. Only Thunder responded with a quiet nicker and a nudge on Marcus's shoulder.

Chapter 4

The following Wednesday started out just fine, from Tommy Valdez's point of view. He hummed along with the tune on the radio as he drove to the track to check on his horses. Pulling up to Barn 7, he noticed Dr. Paige Taylor's truck parked by the barn door. Not alarmed as this was a common sight, he climbed out of his Mazda, clicked the lock on his fob and entered the barn.

The first twinge of concern arrived when he noticed his trainer, Stanley Smithfield, standing in front of Dusty's stall talking in a low whisper to Dr. Taylor.

Valdez approached. "Hey, what's going on?"

Smithfield and Taylor both turned toward him and the

look on their faces, the frowns, the knotted eyebrows, the clenched jaws, showed the concern they were feeling.

"Dusty came out of his stall lame this morning." Smithfield said.

"I'm ordering a complete workup, x-rays," Dr. Taylor said.

Valdez felt his heart start to pound. Not Dusty. Not the answer to his problems. "Wh-what do you think, Doc?" he sputtered.

"I won't know until the tests come back."

Tommy Valdez's silver Mazda negotiated the tight curves of Valley View Drive with practiced ease. But tonight, his hands gripped the wheel so tightly his knuckles had gone white. He had read the veterinary report so many times, he had committed it to memory.

"Complete tear of the suspensory ligament. Bone chips. Career ending."

Eat My Dust—his champion, his golden ticket, his way out—was finished.

He pulled into his driveway just before 1 a.m. The house was dark except for the porch light his wife always left on to welcome him home. She'd be asleep by now, probably tired of waiting up for him.

In his home office, Tommy didn't bother turning on the overhead light, just the desk lamp. He pulled the bourbon from the bottom drawer and poured three fingers into a coffee mug. Downed it in two gulps.

His phone buzzed. Text from Numbers: "Nice party the other night. That horse is a winner. Another race and you're in the money. 2 weeks, Tommy. 50k. Tick tock."

One thing Tommy knew—he couldn't let the vet's report become known or his chance of getting investors would evaporate. He'd have to get that report out of the file in the barn office.

Tommy opened his laptop and pulled up his bank account. $847.23. Saturday's winnings would boost that, but not enough.

Credit cards: $43,000. All maxed.

The syndication deal would work if nobody knew the truth about Dusty. Nobody would buy shares in a lame horse.

He reached for the insurance policy he'd taken out sixteen days ago. $500,000 on Eat My Dust. The agent had tried to talk him into a lower amount—said the premiums on half a million were too steep. But Tommy had insisted. Had known, somehow, that he'd need it.

Just not like this.

He couldn't collect on a lame horse. The insurance company would examine the horse, deny the claim, probably investigate him for fraud.

Unless the body couldn't be examined. Unless…

Tommy stopped that thought before it could fully form. Shook his head. Took another drink.

His hand went to the locked drawer. He knew what was inside—his father's .38 revolver. Some nights, when the debt felt like a noose tightening around his neck, he'd take it out. Hold it. Feel its weight.

Tonight, he didn't even open the drawer.

Picking up his phone again, he noticed a message below the one Numbers had sent. It was from Dianne Brennan, Marcus's wife, thanking him for letting her vent.

Just a week before, she had called, crying. Marcus wouldn't come home until late at night. Spent every evening at the barn with Thunder's Echo. Their marriage was dying, she'd said. She felt like she was losing her mind. Between the tears she had caught her breath and with a new voice, a voice of determination laced with anger, she said she'd do anything—anything—to get her husband back.

He set the phone down and rubbed his face with his hands. He'd heard about Marcus getting thrown out of the house. Everyone in Barn 7 had.

Then his wife's voice drifted down from upstairs. "Tommy? Are you coming to bed?"

He closed the laptop. Put the bourbon away.

"Be right there," he called back.

But as he climbed the stairs, his mind was still turning over problems and possibilities. Numbers's deadline. The insurance policy. Dianne Brennan's desperation.

Desperate times, indeed.

He could only hope the morning would provide him with some answers.

Chapter 5

Nearly a week after the celebration in Barn 7, the jarring beep of his watch alarm pulled JT Walters from sleep. His boots hit the wood floor of the Liberty Racetrack office with a thud that echoed in the empty room. Three in the morning. Again.

He dragged his fingers through his hair and worked his jaw, feeling the stubble scratch against his palm. Being night watchman at a harness racing facility wasn't glamorous. The pay barely covered his mortgage on the little house in the poorer part of town. But in Ashville, Pennsylvania—a town of ten thousand souls tucked between Allegheny ridges—steady work didn't grow on trees…or even on the backs of horses. You took what you could get and thanked the Lord for it.

The coffee on his desk had gone cold hours ago. He left it.

Outside, July heat still clung to the night despite the late hour. Stars scattered across the black canvas above him, thick enough to cast shadows. The irritation that came with interrupted sleep dissolved as he walked. Twenty-five barns stretched across the property. Nearly a thousand Standardbreds sleeping in their stalls, dreaming whatever horses dreamed. Cameras watched the front gate and the grandstand, but the barns? That was his job and he took his responsibility seriously.

In the twenty years he'd worked at the track, nothing ever happened. And certainly not in the seven years he'd been on the night shift. But he liked to think that was because people knew JT Walters was watching.

Barn 1 smelled of hay and leather and warm horse. He moved down the center aisle, stopping to run his hand down a white blaze here, scratch behind an ear there. Soft nickers greeted him. Gentle thuds as horses shifted weight from one leg to another.

All Quiet. All safe.

He stepped back into the night air, turning toward Barn 2 when the first sound reached him.

Distant. Wrong.

The thunder of hooves against wood. Not one horse. Many. The high, piercing screams that came not just from fear, but terror.

Then the smell hit him.

Smoke.

JT ran.

His work boots pounded against the packed dirt and grass as he cut across the lawn. Past Barn 2. Past Barn 3. His lungs burned. His heart hammered against his ribs.

But he didn't slow down.

He rounded the north corner of Barn 4 and his legs locked beneath him.

Barn 7.

The stars had vanished behind a column of smoke—thick and black as oil. Orange light pulsed through the skylights, through every crack in the weathered boards. As he stood frozen, the east wall exploded outward. Flames shot twenty feet in the air, hungry and alive.

He forced himself to move. His hands shook as he pulled his phone from his pocket, nearly dropping it before his trembling fingers managed to unlock the screen.

"9-1-1. What is your emergency?"

The voice was so calm. So impossibly calm.

"Fire!" The word tore from his throat. "Liberty Racetrack in Ashville. Barn 7. Please—the horses—"

He dropped his phone.

The west side. He could get in through the west side. The wind was blowing east. He had time. Maybe.

JT yanked his shirt over his nose and mouth and pulled the barn door open. Heat slammed into him like a breaking ocean wave, dense and suffocating. Smoke poured out, thick and choking. He sucked in one last breath of clean air and plunged inside.

The first stall on the right belonged to Blue River. A brown gelding, five years old and as gentle as a lamb. JT threw open the stall door.

The horse lay sprawled in the straw, sides heaving. JT grabbed the halter from its hook. His eyes streaming. His lungs screaming for air. He dropped to his knees, staying low where the smoke was less dense, and worked the halter over River's head with shaking fingers.

"Come on, boy!" JT stood, hauling on the lead rope. "Get up! River, get up!"

The horse groaned—a sound JT would hear in

nightmares for the rest of his life—and struggled to his feet. Swaying. Confused.

JT pulled him toward the door. Toward air. Toward life.

They burst out together. JT dropped the rope and spun back toward the barn.

Three steps. He made it three steps before the flames exploded through the doorway, roaring as they found fresh oxygen. The force knocked him backward into Blue River. The horse's legs buckled. They went down together in a tangle of limbs.

JT rolled onto his side and pulled his knees to his chest. Wrapped his arms around them. The screaming had stopped.

But the absence was worse than the screaming.

Just the roar of the fire now. The crack and crash of beams giving way. Twenty-seven horses still trapped inside. He'd gotten one out. One.

Twenty-seven others died while he stood outside, helpless.

Sirens wailed in the distance. Red lights strobed across his closed eyelids. Bile rose in his throat. Beautiful animals, trapped in their stalls. Unable to run. Unable to escape. Their final moments filled with heat and smoke and terror.

He wanted to disappear. To dissolve into smoke himself and drift up to those stars.

Instead, he turned and buried his face in Blue River's mane. The horse's breath came in labored gasps, but he was alive. One horse. JT had saved one horse.

But that would never be enough for JT.

News traveled fast in the harness racing community of Ashville, Pennsylvania. Within an hour, vehicles lined both sides of the access road that led from the grandstand to the barns. Owners, trainers, grooms, drivers—

everyone who lived and breathed this life with horses and sulkies descended on Liberty track.

Those whose horses had occupied Barn 7 stalls pushed through the crowd. Their wails cut through the shouts of the firefighters working to contain the blaze. The raw sounds reflected the kind of grief that comes from losing more than property. The kind that comes from losing a partner. Friends. Family.

Water arced from hoses onto Barns 6 and 8, steam rising where it struck the heated walls. Fighting to keep the tragedy contained while grooms pulled horses out of their stalls and led them a safe distance away. Everyone was fighting to prevent the tragedy from spreading like the flames themselves.

Tom Hendricks arrived before dawn, his truck skidding to a stop twenty yards from the command center. He ran through the chaos, calling Blue River's name until someone pointed toward the west side of the property. He found his horse lying in the grass, sides heaving with JT still sitting beside him.

"River." Tom dropped to his knees. "Thank you, God. Thank—"

He stopped. Leaned closer.

The horse's eyes were sealed shut. The lids blistered and swollen. His breathing sounded like wind forcing itself through a crack in a barn door—high pitched and labored.

Tom pulled his phone from his pocket with trembling hands and called Dr. Paige Taylor.

She arrived within minutes, having already left her home after hearing the news of the fire. She examined Blue River in the red glow of the emergency lights while Tom knelt beside her, one hand on his horse's neck.

Her verdict came quietly. Professionally. The heat had seared River's eyes beyond repair. The smoke damage to his lungs was catastrophic. Even if they could save him—and she wasn't certain they could—his quality of life would be nonexistent.

Tom pressed his forehead against Blue River's neck. He nodded once.

JT turned away when Dr. Taylor drew the syringe from her bag. He heard Blue River's breathing ease. Then stop.

Twenty-eight horses.

Chapter 6

As dawn broke over the Allegheny ridges, casting a pale light across the smoking ruins of Barn 7, the questions began.

How had it started?

Where had it started?

Were there smoke detectors? If there were, had they sounded an alarm?

Accusations flew like sparks on the wind. Fingers pointed. Voices rose. The tight-knit community that had celebrated Tommy Valdez's victory with Eat My Dust just days earlier now turned on itself, looking for someone to blame.

But for now, the answers remained buried in the ashes.

With the arrival of daylight came the backstretch people, the ones who rise with the sun and arrive at the barn to feed the horses, muck stalls, clean water buckets, groom their animals and all the other less glamorous responsibilities that go along with horses. But missing was the usual cheerful chatter. On this cloudless day, a dreary pall hung over the remaining twenty-four barns, untouched by the fire but pierced by the pain. Even the horses were quieter than usual, sensing that something was terribly wrong. But horse people know the work must go on, so on it went.

Barn 7 was a pile of smoldering black timbers. What had once been the horse spa, complete with a swimming pool for horse therapy, had recently been converted into a stable. Now it lay in ruins. Curls of steam rose into the air like poisonous snakes. Clusters of mourners gathered behind the yellow and black caution tape. Few spoke above a whisper, most not speaking at all.

In the racetrack's main office, JT sat with his head in his hands, his shoulders shaking as he sobbed.

Frank Morrison, the track security chief and operations manager, and a former volunteer firefighter himself, sat beside him. "Can I get you a cup of coffee?"

JT shook his head. He sniffled, wiping his nose with the back of his hand.

"JT, the state police are here. They need to ask you some questions. Can you do that?" Morrison placed a gentle hand on his employee's shoulder.

JT blew out a long breath of air, lowered his hands, and looked up.

A middle-aged woman with short-cropped brown hair addressed him. "JT, I'm Detective Rita Kowalski from the State Police."

"Ma'am," JT nodded.

"I've come to ask you a few questions." She pulled a chair in front of JT and sat down, pulling out a pocket-sized pad and a pencil. "I realize this must be very difficult for you. I grew up around horses and I understand how much they mean to the people who care for and love them."

JT's eyelids dropped. "They were like family."

"I understand. But as hard as this is, I need to find out from you just what happened last night."

JT blew out another breath. His head rolled back. He shook his head and looked at the ceiling. "I don't know what I can tell you that will be of help."

"Let's start with when you came on duty last evening."

"My usual time, 9 p.m."

Kowalski looked over at Morrison. "Is that what your records show?"

"That's correct. JT is always on time—never misses a day of work."

She turned back to JT. "Please tell me about your routine. What is the first thing you do when you arrive at Liberty?"

"Well, I check in and check the board for any special instructions."

"Were there any?"

"No. Nothing. So, I made my first round inspecting the barns."

"Did you notice anything unusual at that time?"

"No. Nothing unusual. I saw Marcus Brennan driving away from Barn 7. But that happens every night at about this time. He comes to bed down his prized pacer, Thunder's Echo."

"You say he comes every night?"

"Yes. And he has been staying later than usual since his marriage is on the rocks. Lately he has not even been going home. He sometimes bunks at the track dormitory with the grooms." JT took in a shuddering breath. "I can't imagine what he is going through. Thunder's Echo was his pride and joy."

"Anything else?"

"Not at the nine o'clock rounds. Though I was surprised to see Tommy Valdez's car parked near Barn 7. He doesn't usually come by so late."

"Did you talk with him?"

"I didn't see him when I went in the barn to check the horses and when I came back out, his car was gone."

"When you got back to the office, did you see anything on the security cameras that caused you concern?"

"No. Nothing. Of course, they don't cover the stable area, just the front gate and grandstands."

Frank Morrison jumped in. "We have been looking into adding more cameras, but since we have never had any problems, it hasn't been high on our priority list."

"I like to think I have been doing a good job protecting the horses."

Morrison patted JT's shoulder. "And you have. None of this could have been prevented. Fires in stables just happen sometimes. It's no one's fault."

"Unless the fires were intentionally set," said Kowalski.

JT jerked back. "Are you saying this was a case of arson?"

"I'm not saying anything other than that is a possibility we will be investigating. Now let's continue. What about at the next check."

"That would be at midnight."

Kowalski nodded, encouraging him to continue.

JT closed his eyes, collecting his thoughts and replaying the night before. He opened his eyes. "No. There was nothing unusual. I didn't see anyone. The horses were all happy and contented."

"Anything on the camera when you returned to the office?" She looked down at her pad and scribbled notes.

"I saw one car drive by the gates. I only noticed it because I thought it might be the car that belonged to Dianne Brennan. I thought she might be coming to see her husband. The car slowed down but didn't stop so I guess it wasn't her."

"Now let's talk about the three o'clock check. Do you always do your rounds at the same time?"

"No. I change the time occasionally. But I don't vary it by more than half an hour. This time I set my alarm for three o'clock because I wanted to take a short nap." He glanced over at Frank Morrison. "Just a short one. I had a hard day with a sick grandchild."

Morrison frowned.

"So you started your rounds at three instead of two? Is that right?" Kowalski said, urging him on.

"No. Three is my usual time. It's just that Mr. Morrison doesn't want me to sleep between rounds. He wants me to keep an eye on the camera streams."

"Walk me through it." Kowalski poised her pencil. "From the moment you woke up at three."

JT closed his eyes. "I heard the alarm. Got up. Started walking toward Barn 1. Went inside. All was well. I came out and started toward Barn 2." He paused. "That's when I heard it—horses screaming. Not normal sounds. Terror."

"What did you do?"

"I ran." His voice cracked. "I ran as fast as I could, but by the time I got there, the whole east wall was already—" He broke off, his hands trembling.

Kowalski waited, then asked, "Did you see anyone?

Any vehicles?"

JT shook his head. "Nothing. Just flames."

"And you went inside?"

"First, I called 9-1-1 on my cell phone. Then I went in on the west side. I had to try. Blue River was in the first stall." His eyes met hers. "I couldn't leave him."

Kowalski leaned forward and placed her hand on his knee. "You did your best."

She turned to Morrison. "I'm placing a policeman at each gate. They will keep a record of everyone who enters or leaves. The arson investigators will be here as soon as the rubble has cooled enough for them to examine it. No one is to go near the site of the fire. Do you understand?"

"Of course," Morrison said.

Chapter 7

ASHVILLE GAZETTE-BREAKING NEWS

**DEVASTATING FIRE CLAIMS 28 HORSES AT
LIBERTY RACETRACK**
By Paul Coffman

ASHVILLE, PA - Twenty-eight Standardbred horses
perished early this morning when fire consumed Barn
7 at Liberty Racetrack. Track security guard JT Walters
managed to rescue one horse before flames...

Paul Coffman's editor rushed over to his desk,

waving Paul's article over his head. "This is front page material, Coffman. I want daily updates. Human interest. Find out if there's negligence or crime involved."

"I'm already on it," Coffman said.

The white Cadillac Celestiq fishtailed as it skidded to a stop in front of the yellow crime tape that cordoned off Barn 7. Before the engine fully died, Sarah Ferguson threw open the driver's door and launched herself out, leaving the door hanging open behind her. Her designer heels clattered against the asphalt as she ran up to a group of people she knew well—trainers, barn managers, and fellow owners.

The acrid smell of smoke felt heavy in the hot and humid July air. Behind the tape, the skeletal remains of Barn 7 stood like a blackened monument, wisps of gray smoke still curling from the collapsed roof beams. The fire trucks had departed, but their tire tracks left deep ruts in the mud where thousands of gallons of water had been sprayed.

Sarah burst into tears as she reached the group, grabbing the first person she came to and embracing her in a tight hug. Sarah's body shook with sobs as she clung to the woman.

"I can't believe it. I can't believe it!" Sarah's words came out in gasps between tears. "How did this happen? Please tell me—are the horses okay? Did they get out in time?"

The woman she was clinging to held onto Sarah. Her voice cracked. "Sarah, haven't you heard? All the horses died. I'm sorry."

Sarah gasped, her knees buckled slightly. "No!" She yanked herself free from the woman's grasp and shook her head. "That can't be true. Tell me that isn't true. There were twenty-eight horses in that barn!"

"I believe there were thirty, including your mares. I'm

so very sorry, Sarah," her voice breaking completely.

"No. My mares are at my home. I took them home yesterday." She pressed her hand to her chest. "Both of them. They're safe in my barn."

The woman's eyes widened. Fresh tears spilled down her cheeks—this time tears of relief. "Oh, praise the Lord. You have been spared." She pulled Sarah into another embrace. "Thank the heavens you moved them when you did."

"Yes." Sarah pulled back and lowered her voice, glancing toward Frank Morrison who stood twenty feet away, talking grimly to a man who, based upon his uniform, appeared to be the fire marshal. "I have been concerned about both the electrical system and the lack of sprinklers in these barns. I even spoke to management about it—three times in fact." Her voice took on a bitter edge. "But did they listen to me? No! They said I was being paranoid. That the barns had passed inspection. And now look what's happened."

She turned back to her friend and gripped her arm. "Let me give you some advice. Take your horses out, too! Right now! Get them away from here." Sarah's gaze swept across the other barns. "And be grateful it wasn't your barn that went up in flames last night."

Chapter 8

ASHVILLE GAZETTE-SPORTS

**FIRE INVESTIGATION UNDERWAY AT
LIBERTY TRACK**
By Paul Coffman

ASHVILLE, PA - The State Police and Fire Marshal are investigating the cause of the devastating fire at Liberty Racetrack that killed twenty-eight horses the night of July 6th. They are not ruling out arson as the cause of the fire. This reporter learned that one owner had removed her horses the day before the fire. It is unknown if this is connected...

Later that morning, a group of owners converged on Frank Morrison's office beneath the grandstand. The cramped space, already cluttered with filing cabinets, racing forms, and decades of accumulated paperwork, could barely contain the fifteen angry people who pressed inside. The air hung thick with accusation and grief.

Marcus Brennan, his eyes red and puffy, stood at the front, closest to Morrison's desk. His bloodshot eyes were rimmed with red from hours of crying. His normally pressed shirt was wrinkled and smudged with ash. When he spoke, his voice trembled with barely contained rage. "Rumor has it, Frank, that Sarah Ferguson came to you with her concerns about safety issues and you did nothing about it. Is that true?"

Morrison sat stiffly behind his desk, twirling a pen between his fingers—a nervous habit born of years trying to deal with angry horse owners. He cleared his throat. "Yes. Sarah did come to me about the sprinkler system..."

"Or lack thereof," another owner interjected.

Morrison's jaw tightened, but he ignored the comment. "I explained to her that we had put in a $50,000 state-of-the-art sprinkler system in several of the barns a few years ago." He set the pen down and leaned forward, his voice taking on a defensive edge. "But the dust in the air from the hay and shavings kept triggering false alarms. Every other day or so we had fire trucks screaming onto the property, panicking horses, disrupting training schedules, creating all sorts of chaos."

"I remember that mess," said one old-timer. "They were in my barn and a complete nuisance. The fire trucks kept coming for no reason. The Fire Chief finally threatened to never come again until they could see smoke in the sky."

Morrison seized on the validation. "Exactly. So, we had to make the decision to disconnect them. It wasn't that we didn't care—we cared too much to keep a system that was useless at best and dangerous at worst. When you cry wolf that many times, nobody comes when the wolf is real." He looked around the room, assessing the mood. Then added, "We have also asked owners and trainers to not use those big box fans in their horses' stalls as several barn fires across the county have been traced to those."

"Is that what happened here?" Brennan's face flushed darkly. "Was it a fan? I took the fan out of Thunder's stall when you asked. Did everyone else?"

Morrison spread his hands in a gesture of helplessness. "We don't know the cause of the fire, yet. The state police fire marshal will be checking for the cause when the rubble is cool enough. Could be several more days until we know anything."

"That 'rubble,' as you call it, is my horse!" Brennan slapped his palms on the desk as he leaned closer to Morrison. "Thunder wasn't rubble—he was alive yesterday. He had a race scheduled for Saturday. He had—" his voice cracked, and he straightened abruptly, turning away to collect himself.

Morrison's face crumpled. He dropped his head and stared at his hands. "I know," he whispered. For a moment those in the room heard the exhaustion of a man who carried the burden of everyone's loss. "Marcus, I know. It breaks my heart, Thunder, Dusty, all of them."

The room fell silent for a few minutes. The only sound was the hum of the ancient air conditioner laboring in the window.

Then Brennan whirled back around. "And what about Sarah's other complaint, that the electrical is not up to standards?"

Morrison sat up straighter, color rising in his cheeks. "That is categorically and verifiably untrue. That barn has...*had*...the best wiring on the property." He jabbed a finger at the group. "As you all will recall, that building used to house the equine hydrotherapy spa. The electrical system had been set up for that—commercial grade. It was much finer and more elaborate than any of the other barns."

He pulled open a desk drawer and yanked out a folder thick with papers. "I have the inspection reports right here. That system was designed for high-draw equipment—therapy pools, infrared saunas, treadmills. Running some heat lamps and tack room lights? That system could handle that in its sleep." He dropped the folder on the desk with a thud. "So no, this wasn't an electrical issue, I can assure you of that."

A younger woman near the back of the room spoke. Her voice was quiet, hesitant. "Then what was it, Frank? If it wasn't electrical and it wasn't the sprinklers—which weren't even working—then what killed my horse?"

Morrison shook his head and returned to twirling his pen. "We won't know until the inspection is complete."

Chapter 9

Tommy Valdez's silver Mazda CX3 negotiated the tight turns easily as it rocketed up Valley View Drive. Valdez swerved into his driveway at the top of the hill twenty minutes after leaving the track—a trip that normally took thirty-five. Gravel sprayed as he slammed on the brakes. The squealing tires signaled his arrival before he even killed his engine. He burst from the car and sprinted toward the house.

His wife appeared in the doorway; her face creased with concern. She'd been crying—mascara tracks on her cheeks—and she opened her arms wide, ready to hold him, to share the grief of losing Eat My Dust, the horse that promised to be their golden ticket.

Tommy brushed past her outstretched arms without a word. His shoulder knocked against hers as he beelined for the home office.

"Tommy?" His wife's voice was small, confused and hurt. "Tommy, what are you—?"

"Where did I put that insurance policy?" He thumbed through the bottom drawer of his file cabinet. "It must be in here somewhere." He found several files with Dusty's name on them—vet records, race entries, one labeled USTA which held Dusty's registration in the U.S. Trotting Association, and several that held news clippings of the horse's great accomplishments. None of it was what he needed.

Then he remembered. The desk. He spun toward the desk, scattering folders across the floor in his haste. The desktop was a chaos of papers, but right on top—right where he had left it—was the veterinary report. The one he had retrieved from the barn last night. The one that showed the tear on Dusty's ligament. The one that would end Dusty's racing career.

He tossed it aside; it was no longer relevant. He continued searching until he found what he needed: Mutual Assurance Company. Inside the crisp envelope was a life insurance policy on Eat My Dust valued at $500,000 that he had purchased nearly three weeks earlier. He scanned the print. The policy was effective ten days ago.

Tommy sank into his chair, clutching the policy to his chest. His breath came in short gasps.

Behind him, his wife's voice cut through his thoughts. "Tommy. What is that?"

He didn't turn around. Didn't answer. His eyes were fixed on the page, on the number: $500,000. Half a million dollars.

"Tommy." Her voice louder now. "What. Is. That?"

Slowly, he swiveled the chair to face her. "It's insurance on Dusty."

"For how much?"

He hesitated. Then, "Half a million."

His wife gasped. "You bought a half million-dollar insurance policy on Dusty? When?"

"A little over two weeks ago."

The silence that followed was deafening. "Two weeks," she repeated. She uncrossed her arms and took a step into the room. "Two weeks before he died in a barn fire?"

"It's not—" Tommy started.

Her hand flew to her mouth. "Oh, no, Tommy. Tell me you wouldn't. You didn't…"

Tommy opened his mouth, but the words died in his throat. What could he say? That it was a coincidence? That he'd had a premonition? He couldn't tell her the truth: that he was deeply in debt to Joey Castellano. He was planning to sell shares in the valuable horse. But he would never hurt Dusty. He was sure Dusty's racing skills were his ticket out of debt. Now it appeared Dusty's death was his ticket.

Chapter 10

It seemed the phones were ringing louder than usual at the local branch of the Mutual Assurance Company. Located on the third and fourth floors of a high-rise in Philadelphia, about thirty miles from Ashville, the office was always a beehive of activity. While it is true that Fridays were usually busy, they weren't *this* busy.

Carson Schmidt, Chief Claims Officer, heard his assistant answer the phone with the prescribed greeting, "Mutual Assurance Company where we give you the confidence to face life's uncertainties. This is Marta.

How may I help you?"

Soon, Schmidt's desk phone started beeping. All of this was not unexpected on a day when a major catastrophe occurred affecting several of their clients. He heard about the fire at Liberty Racetrack over the radio as he drove to the office.

"Carson Schmidt, how may I help you?"

"Mr. Schmidt, this is Tommy Valdez. I have a policy on my champion harness racing horse for $500,000. I trust you have heard about the fire at Liberty?"

"Yes. Tragic. Truly tragic."

"Yes. Well, my horse Eat My Dust—I lovingly called him 'Dusty'—was one of the casualties. I can't even imagine what he went through, trapped in his stall as he was." Then, without so much as taking a breath, he added, "So I need to report a mortality claim. What documentation do you need from me? What's the claims process?"

"Mr. Valdez, let me look up your policy. But I must tell you that there will be an investigation by the state police."

"What for? It's pretty obvious that there was a fire and that my horse is dead." Irritation crept into his voice.

"Yes. Some things are obvious, to be sure. But the cause of the fire needs to be determined before we can make any payments on claims." Schmidt tapped his pen on his desk. "We will be opening a large-loss file."

"And just how long will that take?" Anger and impatience rose noticeably in Valdez's voice.

"I really can't say. But rest assured, Mutual Assurance will follow up with the state police and keep on top of this. In the meantime, you will need to provide us with any recent vet reports and proof of his value through records of his winnings." Schmidt paused. "Let me add, Mr. Valdez, I am deeply sorry for your loss. I know several people have been affected."

"Well, I'm not concerned about the other people. I just want to collect the money owed to *me,* and the sooner the better!"

The line went dead.

Schmidt pressed the intercom and asked his assistant to bring him the file on Tommy Valdez. A few minutes later he was perusing the contents. Fifteen minutes later he called the extension for one of his insurance investigators.

Callie Oaks was sitting at her desk, wishing she was somewhere else, when her phone rang. "Mutual Assurance investigations team, Callie speaking." Her voice clearly lacked the enthusiasm she knew the company wanted.

"Callie, it's Carson Schmidt."

Callie immediately straightened in her chair. "Yes, Mr. Schmidt." Enthusiasm immediately returned.

"I need you in my office immediately."

"I'll be right there."

Hanging up the phone, Callie ran her fingers through her long, wavy brown hair, grabbed her compact to check her makeup, and stood. She brushed the wrinkles from her skirt and rushed out of her office. When the boss called, she was wise enough to respond quickly.

The attractive young woman was slim, five feet, 7 inches tall. Her green eyes sparkled even when she wasn't thinking about anything in particular. But now she was thinking about a new assignment, and she felt the excitement rising.

She rode the elevator up to the next floor.

When the doors opened, she approached Mr. Schmidt's assistant. "Mr. Schmidt asked me to come see him. Do you know what this is about?"

"It must have something to do with that fire at the track," said the mousy-looking young woman whose name currently escaped Callie.

Callie cocked her head. "I didn't hear anything about that."

"Well, he's up in a tizzy about it. Go on in."

Callie rapped her knuckles on the door.

Schmidt responded with a curt, "Come in."

Entering Schmidt's office brought the familiar butterflies to her stomach. It always meant a new assignment. A new claim to investigate—a good way to end the boredom of paperwork.

She had no idea just how much her life was about to change.

Chapter 11

"Callie, sit down."

"Yes, sir." Callie lowered herself into one of the two leather upholstered chairs facing Schmidt's large contemporary desk, currently covered with files and a large computer screen. She crossed one leg over the other and folded her hands in her lap, trying to exude an air of confidence that she didn't feel. She never did in Schmidt's presence.

Schmidt took a deep breath, his eyes studying her intently.

Callie felt a flutter rising in her chest. She waited for

him to speak first.

"How long have you been with Mutual Assurance?"

"Three years, sir."

"And in that time, you have done an excellent job as an investigator."

"Thank you, sir," she said, feeling only the slightest amount of relief.

He clutched his hands and lowered them to the desk. "I seem to recall from our first interview that you had been very involved in harness racing growing up."

"I was raised in a harness racing family in Ohio. I've put in my time in the sulky." She smiled, trying to lighten the mood and calm her nerves.

"That's good, because I have an important assignment for you. But, unlike your other investigations, this one will need to be undercover."

"Undercover, sir?" Her eyebrows knitted. She tilted her head to one side.

"Let me explain." Schmidt leaned back in his chair. "I assume you have heard about the fire at Liberty Racetrack."

"Only just now from…um—" his assistant's name suddenly coming to her— "Marta."

"Well, we are up to our eyeballs in liability *if* this was an accident."

"If?"

"From what I've learned, the state police have not determined a cause and won't for at least a few more days. It's still too hot to send in investigators."

Callie nodded.

"But I want to be ahead of the game here. I want boots on the ground immediately. But not visibly. I want you to get a job at the track. With your background, you're perfect for this assignment. You can work behind the scenes and find out what's really going on. I'll pull some strings and get you in. Be ready to show up at the track office bright and early Monday morning."

By Saturday, the charred remains of Barn 7 had cooled enough for the inspectors to start sifting through the damage. Large equipment was brought in to lift the timbers and set them to one side. Then, the owners and trainers, friends and sympathizers, along with the curious, watched as, one by one, the burnt remains of twenty-seven horses were lifted out of the rubble. Blue River's body had been removed on the first day. It was a heart-wrenching sight.

It was impossible to tell one horse from the next, so every horse brought everyone to tears as if it were their own.

Several large trucks with open beds waited to receive the bodies and take them to a local pet cemetery which had made a munificent donation by providing the space for the burial of the beloved animals. Several members of the United States Trotting Association (USTA) and the Pennsylvania Harness Horsemen's Association (PHHA) pooled their money and purchased a bronze memorial plaque to be placed at the site. The words on the memorial read:

"In remembrance of 28 noble souls lost to fire on July 6, 2026. These Standardbred horses lived with purpose, ran with heart, and are forever cherished. May they find endless pastures beyond."

Once the horses had all been removed, fire and police investigators started carefully combing through the wreckage, looking for the cause of the fire. Early in the afternoon, accelerant-sniffing dogs were brought in. Regardless of how many questions were thrown at them by the dozens of people watching, the investigators refused to answer and went about their work with all seriousness.

"The fire marshal will hold a press conference when we have finished our investigation," one of the officers said as he walked under the caution tape and pushed through the crowd.

That night, a press conference was held. The remains of Barn 7 were the backdrop.

The state fire marshal was the primary speaker.

"Ladies and gentlemen of the press and owners and trainers connected to the tragedy at Barn 7, as the State Fire Marshal, it is my duty to express our sincere condolences at the loss of your treasured animals. The entire State of Pennsylvania mourns with you.

"I've called this press conference tonight to report the results of our investigation as to the cause of the fire." He paused for a moment, surveying the expectant expressions on the faces of the dozens of people who stood before him.

"Let me first explain a little background." He removed his hat and dabbed his forehead with his handkerchief. "The most common causes of barn fires are electrical."

Sarah Ferguson, who was standing near the front, glared at Frank Morrison.

The fire marshal continued. "Often the wiring is unprotected and thus open to damage from rodents. Or, perhaps, extension cords have been used and then damaged. Some electrical appliances such as fans, accumulate dust and can create sparks which can cause a fire. Even hay can burst into flames in what we call spontaneous combustion. This happens when hay is wet and generates heat as it decomposes. That is why we recommend storing hay in a separate barn at least one hundred feet away from the stable where the horses are housed."

"But none of those things caused this fire," shouted Morrison from the side of the crowd. His tone of voice indicated he felt threatened and thus, defensive. Sarah Ferguson huffed.

"You are correct," acknowledged the fire marshal. "I just want you to know how thorough we are being in our investigation. We eliminated all of the usual causes before we ever brought in the dogs."

"Dogs?" said one spectator.

"Yes. We have trained arson dogs that can sniff out an accelerant, such as gasoline, if such was used."

"Did they find anything?" called out another person in the crowd.

"Yes."

Shock rumbled through the crowd.

"You're saying the fire was started on purpose?" a woman said.

"Yes. That is what I'm saying."

"No way!" shouted Tommy Valdez. "That's not possible. No one around here would intentionally start a fire. We love…loved…our horses. They were extremely valuable. No one would want to kill them!" His histrionic outburst drew attention from everyone in the crowd.

"He's right." Several people added their agreement.

Yet others remained quiet, scanning the faces of the people around them.

Paul Coffman tucked his notebook and pencil in his pocket and rushed to his truck.

Chapter 13

ASHVILLE GAZETTE-BREAKING NEWS

STATE FIRE MARSHAL CONFIRMS ARSON AT LIBERTY RACETRACK
By Paul Coffman

ASHVILLE, PA – The state fire marshal confirmed that the fire at Liberty Racetrack on July 6th was the result of arson. No suspects or motive have been identified by the state police who are continuing...

Paul's editor at the Ashville Gazette clapped him on

the shoulder as he returned to the office. "Great job on this story. The whole town is eating it up. Keep the news coming."

Callie Oaks woke up before her alarm. Looking at the clock she groaned as she focused on the numbers that greeted her—4:30.

"I could have slept for another half hour," she grumbled. She knew there was no point trying to go back to sleep. She was too keyed up. It was Monday, the day she was to take on a new identity and a new job as an undercover investigator.

She went to her closet and pulled out some comfortable jeans and a crisp, yellow blouse. She had dug her barn boots out of storage the night before. Her nerves were on edge as she struggled to keep her hands from shaking while she put on a touch of blush and a little mascara. The barn was no place for a lot of makeup, but it never hurt to take advantage of her natural beauty. Blowing out a long breath, she tied her hair into a ponytail. Sitting on the edge of her bed, she pulled on her boots and left her room for the thirty-minute drive to Ashville.

Arriving at the track well before 6:00 a.m., Callie pulled her car up to the back side of the grandstand near the door labeled "OFFICE." She stepped onto the pavement, clicked the lock button on her fob and listened for the beep. Then, she walked to the door, took a deep breath, and entered the racetrack office.

Frank Morrison greeted her as she entered and escorted her into his office. It was a small, windowless room tucked beneath the stadium seating. A lamp, sitting on an untidy desk cast a sterile glow around the room, lighting the numerous photos of harness racers pulling their sulkies and drivers, while others depicted a driver standing in the Winner's Circle beside a horse while holding a trophy. Callie quickly recognized the man in the photo as a much younger Frank Morrison.

"Glory days gone by."

"You were a driver?"

"Ancient history."

"You're not that old. Why did you quit?"

"You *are* an investigator, aren't you?" Morrison said with half a smile.

"Sorry. I shouldn't pry."

Morrison brushed that aside. "I'll just say, I lost my nerve but never the love of the horses. That's why I want to get to the bottom of this. I've agreed to help Carson's investigation."

Morrison motioned for her to take a seat in a straight-backed wooden chair set to the side of his desk. As soon as she was seated, he looked her in the eye. "I'll be your contact here at the track—your go-between with Carson." He held up a file. "We have put together a false identity for you. You are now Haylie Norr from Ohio. You have a lot of experience as an exercise driver to take the trotters and pacers for a jog. You will be working with the trainers in Barn 6 and Barn 8. They have already been informed that you are coming and that you are extremely experienced." He paused. "You *are*, aren't you?"

"Yes, Sir. I can handle that."

"Good. Good. Your job will be to help with the horses anytime and anywhere there is a need. But the most important thing is to keep your eyes and ears open. Build trust with the owners and trainers. We are hoping if anyone knows anything about this fire, they will feel comfortable opening up to you. You are a newcomer, so we are hoping they won't feel threatened by you as they would with myself or Carson."

"I understand."

"Now, go make yourself a part of the community. Report anything you hear, no matter how small or seemingly insignificant it may seem. I will relay it to Carson."

"Where are the police and fire inspectors in their investigation?"

"The area is still off limits to everyone but their investigators. They have concluded that arson was involved."

"They know that for a fact?" Callie leaned toward Morrison, her eyebrows raised.

"Yes. They say there is no doubt about that. They are now in the process of analyzing burn patterns on the structure and debris to determine the fire's point of origin. They are testing for remnants of accelerants and ignition sources."

"So, we really are looking for an arsonist?" Callie rubbed her forehead. The thought of someone intentionally killing all those horses was almost too much for her to accept.

"That does mean the track was not negligent in any way. While that validates me and my staff, it is small consolation when you consider the tremendous loss we all suffered when those poor horses died."

"Seems to me you have some culpability regarding security."

Morrison stiffened. "We are hiring a company to see what we can do to tighten our security. We have never had any issues before. We believed that the cameras we have installed plus the security guard that makes his rounds at night was enough," Morrison said, his face tightening, his hands clutched.

"But it wasn't."

"Sadly, that is true."

"And what about the people who had policies with my company? With Mutual Assurance?"

"That will depend upon your findings." Morrison
stood to escort her out.

54

Chapter 14

Barn 6 was abuzz with activity, typical for any racetrack in the early morning. Morrison and Callie entered through the main aisleway to see grooms feeding, cleaning, and in various stages of harnessing. Dust motes danced in the shafts of sunlight streaming in through the high windows above the stalls. Callie breathed in the heady scent of horses and barns, so familiar to her from her upbringing. She smiled. It was good to be out of an office and back with the horses. For a brief moment, she questioned why she had ever left this world.

"Tommy, this is the new exercise driver I told you about. Meet Haylie Norr from Ohio."

Valdez turned from preparing a stall for the arrival of one of his horses. After the fire in Barn 7, he moved his operation into Barn 6 where there were empty stalls. He eyed the young woman with a certain degree of skepticism. "Are you sure she knows what she's doing? I'm not in any mood to take chances with a newbie right now."

Callie stepped forward and extended her hand. "Mr. Valdez, it is a pleasure to meet you. Let me first express my deepest condolences at the loss of Eat My Dust. He was such a magnificent horse with a very promising future."

"Indeed," mumbled Valdez without taking her hand.

Callie lowered her hand but didn't back down. "Let me assure you that I am very experienced with harness racing, having been involved with it all my life. I would be grateful if you would trust me as a jogger with your horses."

"Trust must be earned, young lady."

"I'm aware of that and I intend to earn your trust and prove to you that I know what I am doing." She offered him a warm smile. He didn't return it.

"We shall see."

Callie lifted her chin and looked Valdez in the eye. "Does that mean you will give me a try?" She suddenly felt the heat and humidity of the July day pressing down upon her.

"I have a two-year-old filly coming from my farm to the track in a few minutes. She will need a jog around the track to get familiar with her new surroundings. We'll see how you do."

Not ten minutes had elapsed before a two-horse trailer pulled up beside the barn and a bay filly was backed out the rear door. Callie felt excitement crackling through her limbs as she gazed at the beautiful filly. How good it was to be around horses again.

Callie approached the filly, feeling Valdez's eyes on her. She spoke to the horse in a whisper, while looking her in the eye. There was kindness there, to be sure, but also a touch of fear at her new surroundings. "Hello little lady. It's alright. You're safe here with me." She turned to Valdez. "What do you call her?"

"Sunny, for There's a Sunset."

Callie remembered that naming rules limit the number of letters and spaces in a racer's name to thirty. She mentally counted the letters. There's a Sunset. Just sixteen.

Taking her lead rope, she led There's a Sunset up and down the length of the barn, talking to her the entire time. Next, she led her to the track and walked her along the outside pylons. Several horses were being jogged, pulling their sulkies and drivers along the outside of the track at a slow, calm trot. The filly's head went up and ears twisted forward and back, but she offered no resistance. "That's a good girl. What a good girl you are, Sunny," Callie crooned in a sing-song voice.

On the inside of the track, a colt dashed past. Callie recognized the horse as a "Free-legger"—a pacer that races without wearing hobbles to connect the lateral legs. Suddenly, the colt broke his stride and started to gallop.

Sunny stopped and watched the horse and sulky bolt toward the outside. She snorted, then began to prance in a circle around Callie. Callie remained calm, walking beside her around the circle until Sunny stopped and snorted again. Her head remained up, ears pointing toward the wayward horse, now far down the track.

"That's a girl, Sunny. Nothing to worry about. Let's keep walking."

It took several strides before Sunny was ready to return to a calm walk beside Callie. But eventually, the filly relaxed.

Returning to Barn 6, Callie caught a whiff of wet, burnt rubble wafting on the breeze coming from Barn 7. Sunny's nostrils flared. "It's okay, Sunny. You're safe."

She led the filly to Valdez. "Let's get her bedded down in her stall and feed her. Tomorrow is soon enough to harness her. I'll take her for another walk this afternoon."

Valdez didn't comment but turned on his heel and led the way to Sunny's stall. Callie smiled to herself, knowing she had passed the first test.

Chapter 15

The next morning, Callie arrived at the track before dawn. She parked near Barn 6, relieved to find the lot empty—no other backside workers or grooms had arrived yet. The air still held the acrid bite of smoke.

She crossed the gravel drive separating her barn from what remained of Barn 7. Yellow caution tape ringed the charred skeleton of the structure, but something new caught her eye: a second barrier of tape, bold black letters spelling out "Crime Scene." Her pulse quickened. She pulled out her phone and snapped several photos for

Carson Schmidt.

Circling to what had been the barn's entrance, Callie stopped short. Someone had created a makeshift memorial—a sprawl of flowers, balloons, and handwritten notes weighted down against the morning breeze with bricks and stones. She stood silent for a moment, thinking of the twenty-eight Standardbreds who'd been stabled here just days ago. The magnificent horses who'd never left.

A prayer formed wordlessly in her mind.

Her gaze drifted back to the rubble—twisted metal, blackened timber, the ghost of what had been. The devastation felt both surreal and viscerally present, the encroaching light making every detail too sharp.

Footsteps crunched on the gravel behind her.

Callie turned as a young man approached.

"Do you work here?" he asked.

Callie examined the stranger who had approached her. She judged him to be about her age, but a bit taller and a good deal stockier. Light reddish hair crowned a handsome face. Blue eyes sparkled when he smiled, which he was doing now.

"Ummm…yes. I'm new. Just started yesterday."

He extended his hand which she took. "I'm Paul Coffman. I'm a reporter for the *Ashville Gazette*."

"Nice to meet you. I'm Ca—Haylie Norr. I'm working for a few of the owners and trainers."

"Who might that be?"

"Well, Tommy Valdez, so far."

"Aww. The owner of Eat My Dust."

"Yes. At least he *was*," she said as an ache suddenly captured her heart.

"Tragic loss. That one was sure to be a champion. Headed for the Pacing Triple Crown, I heard. I'm wondering if he was insured."

"I'm sure I don't know, but it wouldn't surprise me

considering his value.”

“How much do you think he was valued at?”

“Again, I would only be guessing, but I’d have to say many hundreds of thousands of dollars.”

“That would be only if he remained healthy.”

“Of course.” Callie was curious as to where this was going. “Do you have reason to believe that he wasn’t healthy at the time of the fire?”

“I’ve just heard rumors.” Coffman raised his eyebrows.

“What sort of rumors?” Callie was careful not to sound too eager.

“Just some things about drugging horses. I’m trying to get more information before I publish anything, of course.”

“Of course.”

“Hey, perhaps we can work together.”

“How so?” Callie raised her eyebrows.

“Well, you’ll be very hands-on with the horses and trainers. If you hear or see anything untoward, I would appreciate being the first to know. My editor wants follow-up stories on the fire investigation’s progress, but I’m hitting dead ends—I could use some help.”

Callie suddenly realized this reporter might come in handy. “I can do that on one condition.”

“Which is?” he asked, his blue eyes sparkling.

“That you keep me informed of any tidbits about the fire that you pick up. I don’t want to get myself in a situation where I might get in trouble by association.”

“Good point.” The reporter extended his hand for a second time and smiled. “It’s a deal, partner.”

There is much to be read in a smile, and Callie liked what she was reading.

Chapter 16

"Are you Haylie Norr?"

Callie, not accustomed to being called by that name, kept walking down the aisle between the stalls.

"Excuse me. Are you Haylie?"

Callie jerked to a stop, suddenly realizing it was she who was being addressed. *Oh my gosh,* she thought, *I have to get better at this undercover stuff.* She took a deep breath to gain her composure, plastered a smile on her face, and turned. Walking toward her was a tall, slim man, she guessed in his forties. Maybe even fifties. His face was pleasant, though not particularly handsome by her standards, his jaw a mite too chiseled.

"Yes, I am. I'm sorry, my mind was elsewhere."

"I'm Stanley Smithfield, Tommy Valdez's trainer and driver."

"Oh, I'm so pleased to meet you." Callie's face reddened. *Not a great way to make a good first impression,* she thought.

"I understand Tommy has you working with the new filly."

"Sunny. Yes. But I am here to do whatever you, as her trainer, want me to do."

"Good. Good. I don't have time to do all the driving myself. And, with the young ones, I like to start slow."

"That's great. I'll do whatever you ask of me…as long as it's kind, of course."

"Of course. Today, let's just see how she takes to the harness."

Callie felt Smithfield's eyes on her as she haltered Sunny and led her out of the stall. "Does she cross-tie?"

"I guess we'll find out," Smithfield said.

"I'd rather be safe than sorry." Callie led Sunny up to the cross-ties, two chains hanging down on either side of the aisle. But instead of using those, she attached two lead ropes to the filly, one on either side of her halter, and tied the lead ropes with safety knots to the rings on the posts. Callie glanced over at Smithfield and was pleased to see a look of approval on his face.

After grooming Sunny, Callie went into the tack room and picked up a light-weight harness. Piece by piece, she put the harness on the filly, adjusting the crupper and numerous straps just right.

"Do you want to check my work?" she asked Smithfield, who was leaning against a stall door watching her work.

"Not necessary, Haylie. You've done a splendid job.

Let's put on the open bridle without blinders."

Once the harness and bridle were in place Callie stood back and admired her work. Sunny had not resisted in the least. "I guess she has already been introduced to all this paraphernalia." She smiled as she stroked Sunny's neck.

"It appears so. I appreciate the kind manner in which you handled her. Especially being unfamiliar with the horse. Let's lead her out and see how she does attached to a jog cart."

Callie unhooked the make-shift cross-ties and followed Smithfield out of the barn, Sunny walking calmly beside her.

The racing sulkies, that Smithfield called "race bikes," and jog carts were lined up under an overhanging roof. The two types of carts were easy to tell apart. The jog carts were heavier, more solid, some even having a wide seat that would hold two drivers. These were built for training and conditioning.

The sulkies were of a much finer, lighter and more aerodynamic design. Everything about them said they were built for speed.

Smithfield stopped in front of one of the jog carts that could hold two people.

"We'll test her out with one of these so I can ride with you, Haylie. I want to see how you do driving."

"Of course. Makes sense to me."

She stood at Sunny's head as the trainer brought the cart up to the filly from behind. Once he had her standing between the shafts, he hooked each one to the metal quick hitches on the sides of the surcingle part of the harness. Each task was completed calmly while Smithfield kept up a running commentary to the horse about what a good, smart girl she was. Sunny clearly responded well to such treatment.

Once the second shaft was attached to the harness, he approached her head on the right side. Slipping a sugar cube out of his pocket, he fed her a treat. "Let's take her for a walk," he said when finished.

With Callie on one side, and Smithfield on the other, they led Sunny toward the track. As Sunny felt the weight of the jog cart pulling against the harness, her ears swiveled back, and her body tensed. Smithfield clucked and applied gentle pressure on the lead he had attached to the bit. Sunny took a tentative step forward. Then another and another. The cart began rolling behind her. Her pace evened out, and though her neck remained slightly arched with alertness, her breathing stayed steady. By the end of that first trip around the mile-long track, the filly's head and neck had relaxed from its initially high carriage, and there was an unmistakable spring in her step that suggested she was beginning to enjoy this new challenge.

Callie glanced over at Smithfield and noticed the look of satisfaction on his face. Then she looked at Sunny and couldn't help but smile.

It was early afternoon, and Callie was relaxing in the barn office when Tommy Valdez entered. She jumped to her feet, her heart quickening.

"Sit down, young lady. From what I hear, you deserve a rest. You have been working hard." Tommy's slick, black hair reflected the stark white glare of the panel of fluorescent lights in the ceiling. "Stanley told me he is very impressed with you. Says you really know what you're doing."

A wave of relief flowed through her, and she released the breath she had been holding in a huff.

Valdez chuckled. "Do I scare you that much, young Haylie?"

Callie couldn't help but smile. "No. It isn't you. I always feel a need to prove myself at a new job. I'm glad you and Mr. Smithfield are liking my work."

"Sit," he repeated.

Sitting on the edge of the well-worn loveseat with its plaid upholstery that had once been quite fashionable, she leaned forward, resting her elbows on her knees and clutching her hands. She waited for Valdez to speak.

"Stan and I have decided to put you in charge of working with Sunny. I've already told Morrison I want to hire you as my assistant trainer. He can find another groom-exercise driver to take your place if other trainers need help."

Callie didn't conceal the smile that spread across her face. She figured she'd still have access to everything and everyone she needed for her investigation. Maybe this would even give her more credibility.

"That's wonderful news, Mr. Valdez."

"Time to call me Tommy, young lady."

"Tommy," she corrected.

The creak of the door opening on rusty hinges interrupted their conversation.

"You aren't trying to hide from me, are you?" a muscular man's frame filled the doorway.

Valdez stood quickly. "Numbers," he stammered. "Of course not. I'm just meeting with my new assistant trainer."

Callie couldn't help but notice the shaking in his voice and the beads of sweat that suddenly appeared on his forehead.

The imposing man walked in, filling the room with an air of tension.

"Let me introduce you to Miss Haylie Norr. Haylie, this is Joey Castellano. He likes to hang around the track."

Castellano chuckled under his breath but shook Callie's hand and offered her a smile. "It's my pleasure, young lady." His dark eyes locked into hers with an almost unnerving intensity. He looked over at Valdez.

"You're picking them young and pretty, I see."

"She has a great way with horses. And she knows what she is doing holding the lines."

Castellano turned back to Callie and winked. "Yes, I'm sure she does."

Feeling discomfort creeping through her body, Callie pulled her hand away. "It's a pleasure to meet you as well," she lied. "Why did Mr. Valdez, er…Tommy, call you 'Numbers?'"

"I have a certain skill, you see." Addressing Valdez again, he said, "Well, I didn't come here to meet your lovely new trainer. We have a business matter to discuss, Tommy."

Valdez hustled Castellano out the door before saying anything else. Callie followed and peeked down the aisle just in time to see the two men disappear around the corner of the barn. She couldn't hear what they were saying, but both men were clearly animated.

Callie determined to ask Frank Morrison about this new man in the picture. She walked to the track office where she found Morrison at his desk talking on the phone. He looked up as she tapped on his door.

"I have to go." Morrison abruptly ended his call. "Miss Norr, what can I do for you?" He set down his phone.

"I have a question for you."

"All right. Ask away."

"Who is Joey Castellano?"

Morrison sat up straighter and folded his arms across his chest. "Castellano is the local backstretch bookie. Everyone calls him 'Numbers.' He accepts bets on the races here at Liberty."

"Is it legal?" Callie asked.

"I won't tell you it's legal," he said, running one hand through his hair. "But it's been going on as long as I've been here, and it's not my job to police it. I figure no one is forcing people to bet on the outcome of a race. The legal betting is the pari-mutuel betting going on in the clubhouse."

"Is there ever any fraud involved?"

Morrison let out a huff. "Let's put it this way: if a bookie is a shyster, the word gets around pretty fast, and no one will do business with him."

"Did Tommy Valdez do business with him?"

"I can't say for sure. I *have* heard rumors that Tommy is a gambling man."

Chapter 17

Callie relished the feeling of the wind in her hair as she sat in the jog cart behind Sunny. The morning sun warmed her back as she jogged the filly around the outer edge of the Liberty racetrack. She held the lines gently in her hands, letting the horse tell her when to lighten the contact and when to put more pressure on her. Sunny was going to be trained as a pacer, as nearly eighty percent of the Standardbreds in North America are because they can better balance themselves going around the tighter, shorter tracks found here.

But right now, Callie's job was just to build up her

strength and expose her to the track. A horse that is easily spooked is more likely to break from the trot and start cantering or galloping. She had to be exposed to as many new things as possible before the training to pace began.

As Callie guided the filly around the track, she wondered why she had ever left this life in the first place.

She jogged Sunny past the grandstand and glanced over at Smithfield. He lifted his chin in acknowledgment, and she responded with a smile and a lift of her hand. Before they were past, she noticed Valdez approach. *Good,* she thought. *He can see for himself that I know what I'm doing.*

No sooner had the thought crossed her mind than another horse and driver team came up beside them at a fast clip, passing them on the left.

Sunny, startled, broke into a canter.

Callie braced her feet in the stirrup bars of the cart and pulled back on the lines. "Whoa girl. Whoa Sunny."

In just a few strides, Callie had the filly back under control and into a calm jog again.

"There's a girl, Sunny. That's why we're out here— to get you used to all this." But Callie was secretly pleased with the filly's reaction to being passed. She clearly had an instinct to race. That was a good sign.

Finishing the workout, Callie brought the filly down to a leisurely walk and directed her back to Barn 6. As she set about removing the harness her work was interrupted.

"Nice driving."

Callie turned. There was that reporter's smile again. "Thanks, Paul." She returned his smile.

"Say, I hear there is a memorial service for the horses that died in the fire. It's over at the burial site." He looked down and shuffled his feet like a schoolboy. "I thought you might be interested in going."

Callie instantly realized this would be the perfect

opportunity to see all the people connected to the fire. And the opportunity to spend time with this charming journalist was not lost on her either. "I'd love to go. Thanks for inviting me."

<h1 style="text-align:center">Chapter 18</h1>

Callie sat beside Paul as they drove through the now-familiar town of Ashville. Nestled in the rolling hills west of Philadelphia, it still had that traditional Pennsylvania feel: a few blocks of two- and three-story brick buildings housed local shops, a café with a permanent "OPEN" sign in the window, and a hardware store that had been family-owned for generations. They passed the small-town square which was anchored by a WWI memorial and the old, county courthouse. The newer development stretched toward the edges of town where former farmland had given way to shopping centers and chain restaurants.

Beyond the town, rolling hills dotted with farms and wooded areas recalled the peaceful aura of days gone by.

Paul chatted amiably as they passed over the occasional creek and small rivers that helped determine where this town was first settled centuries ago. "Ashville is one of the oldest towns west of Philly. There are lots of old timers still around who love to tell stories from the olden days. Some are pretty wild."

Their destination was an old farm that had been converted to a peaceful pet cemetery. The property displayed a distinctly Pennsylvania look. An old farmhouse that rested atop a native fieldstone foundation and sported a wraparound porch was nestled among mature oak and maple trees. A tilting carriage house, in need of a fresh coat of paint, was tucked behind the main house. It was here that Paul pulled into a parking spot, his small pickup truck snuggling easily between the larger pickups and SUVs.

A summer drizzle was wilting the already anguished spirits of the large crowd gathered at the pet cemetery. Callie was surprised at the size of the group that had come to memorialize the twenty-eight horses who had died so tragically. She had set the goal to meet every owner and trainer involved with Barn 7. This was going to be more difficult than she imagined. She tucked her arm through Paul's. "Would you recognize the owners of the horses?"

"Sure. I've hung around enough to know them."

"I would appreciate it if you would point them out to me. I want to express my condolences."

"Of course." He patted her hand that was holding his arm.

As Callie and Paul approached the gathering from one side, a silence hung over the crowd, the kind that comes when words feel inadequate. Some huddled under umbrellas; others wrapped their arms tighter around their jackets, lifting collars and adjusting baseball caps.

Callie noticed Tommy Valdez standing with Stanley Smithfield and a woman near Callie's age she didn't know. She worked her way over to them.

Valdez turned when she touched his arm. "Haylie," he said with a smile. "I'm glad you came."

"Good to see you, Haylie," Smithfield said over Valdez's head. "Have you met Dr. Paige Taylor, our veterinarian?"

Callie turned and looked into the pleasant face of the woman standing beside them. Her hair was set in a braid that hung down her back and her skin was the color of bronze, the result of many hours out in the sun. Crow's feet accentuated her eyes when she smiled, which she was doing now, warmly.

"It's a pleasure to meet you, Haylie." Her voice was crisp, almost masculine.

"The pleasure is mine," Callie responded. "Oh, and this is Paul Coffman. He brought me here. I'm not sure I could have found it on my own."

"Yes. We've met. The reporter." She returned her gaze to Callie.

"New to the area?" Taylor asked.

"Yes. I'm from Ohio."

"Ah, harness racing country that."

"It's in my blood, so to speak," Callie said, truthfully.

Dr. Taylor turned back to Valdez. "As I was saying, I seem to have misplaced Dusty's file. It isn't in your office where I usually leave it. Keep an eye out, will you?"

"Of course, of course. I'll let you know if I find it."

Dr. Taylor stepped away.

A voice speaking into a scratchy microphone cut through the air, interrupting the somber occasion. "Ladies and gentlemen, friends and neighbors, welcome. I'm sorry that we have to gather under these horrific circumstances, but I'm glad you could come to honor the twenty-eight magnificent horses who lost their lives two weeks ago. In case you don't already know me, I am John Stanton, the president of the Pennsylvania Harness Horsemen's Association. I want to personally thank the Old Friends Pet Cemetery and the United States Trotting Association for their generosity in helping us provide this burial site and lovely memorial for our old friends."

He paused while applause rippled through the crowd. Callie sensed that no one really felt like celebrating anything, but they knew they needed to express their gratitude. She admired that.

"We thought it would be most appropriate to have an open mic where anyone who wants to share their thoughts can have the time to speak," the president said. "So, I will sit down and turn the time over to all of you."

For the first few minutes, everyone just stood in awkward silence. Callie looked around at the crowd. Most stood with eyes downcast, clutching umbrellas or one another. Then one of the youngest drivers stepped up to the mic.

With a quiver in his voice, he began to speak. "I am having such a hard time dealing with my grief at losing WindintheWillows. She was the best trotter I ever sat behind. You all know Willow was smaller than the others, but she had the biggest heart. She never gave up." His voice caught. He cleared his throat. "I don't know what else to say except that I am going to miss her and I'll never forget her."

An owner stepped up and talked about the colt he lost. "I bred Over the Hill. I was there when he was born. I watched him stand up for the first time on those spindly legs then crumple back down to the straw." He smiled and a reverent chuckle rippled through the crowd. "He wasn't always the easiest colt to train."

"I can attest to that!" a man shouted out.

"Yes, I know, Walt. You earned your money on Hilly, that's for sure. But he always loved a good race."

Now that the ice had broken, several more people stepped up to the mic to share stories about their horses. A grizzled trainer with calloused hands took the microphone and talked about Midnight Runner. "Could be ornery as a she-goat. Bit me twice. Kicked me once. But he'd trot his heart out every single race." He wiped his eyes. "I'd take another bite if I could have him back."

One by one they came—owners, trainers, drivers—each adding their grief to the collective memorial.

Just as Callie thought the comments had run their course, Marcus Brennan stepped up to the mic. Callie didn't know his name but had noticed him standing in the center with his arm around a beautiful young woman who was several inches shorter than he was.

Without preamble the young man began. "The last two weeks have been a time of self-reflection for me. You all know me as 'The Rookie.'" More polite chuckles. "I never minded the nickname because I knew it was true. I didn't just dabble with horse ownership and harness racing; I jumped in with two feet and gave it all I had. Thunder's Echo became the entire focus of my life. I quit my job to be with him. I quit my life."

He rubbed his eyes with both hands before continuing. "Sadly, I almost gave up the most important thing of all…" His voice choked… "my sweet wife." He took a deep breath. "The last two weeks have taught me that I need to keep my priorities in order. You won't be seeing me around the track anymore. I'm hanging up my sulky."

He left the mic and wrapped his arms around his wife, who was sobbing.

"Who is that?" Callie whispered to Paul.

"Marcus Brennan. He lost a very promising four-year old stallion. The horse was doing great in his four-year-old season and seemed to have a promising future as a stud. Before this happened, his marriage was on the rocks. He was pretty much living at the track."

"Well, maybe something good came of tragedy," Callie said.

Paul shrugged. "High price for everyone to pay to save a marriage."

"Yeah. Don't you wish there could have been another way?"

Paul nodded.

The drizzle stopped and the umbrellas came down, making it easier for Callie to see faces. "Introduce me around," she said, tugging on Paul's sleeve.

The first person they approached was a petite, well-dressed woman of about fifty. "Haylie Norr, I'd like to introduce you to Sarah Ferguson. Sarah is the queen bee around here that keeps everything buzzing."

Ferguson patted him on the arm, enjoying the compliment, even as she said, "Oh, Paul, you give me too much credit." Turning to Callie, she said, "Is Paul your beau?"

Callie blushed. "Oh, no. I just met him at the track. I'm an assistant driver for Mr. Valdez."

"Tommy has you working for him? Well, you must be talented. I'll have to talk him into sharing you."

"Let me say, I am so very sorry for your loss," Callie said.

"Oh, sweetie, I was the lucky one. Just by chance, I had moved my two mares home the very day before the fire."

Callie blinked in surprise. She hadn't heard that anyone had taken their horses out right before the fire. Gathering her composure, she said, "I'm so happy to hear that. Tell me. Why did you take them home?"

Ferguson looked around. Noticing Frank Morrison

standing nearby, she leaned in toward Callie. "Truth be told," she said in a whisper, "I was concerned about my mares' safety in that barn. It breaks my heart to be proven right."

Chapter 19

On the drive home, Paul chattered while Callie sat quietly, making a mental list of the people she had met and her impressions of each of them. No one struck her as the kind that would purposely kill twenty-eight horses.

When Paul took a breath, Callie jumped in. "Thank you for taking me and introducing me to so many people. You really have a gift of gab!"

Paul chuckled. "I can talk a bear out of his cave in winter!"

Callie snorted. "I didn't know you were an expert on hibernation."

"Just one of my many talents."

Callie probed. "Are you going to write a story about the people who shared their feelings at the memorial? That should please your editor who wants the human-interest angles."

Coffman shrugged. "Maybe. But I'm kind of curious about Sarah Ferguson and why she moved her horses just before the fire. I think I'll follow up with her."

Then he changed the subject. "Say, would you like to stop for some dinner?"

Callie hesitated. She didn't know why. She just hadn't expected Paul to ask her on a date. At the same time, she feared developing a relationship under false pretenses. She was liking Paul's company…maybe too much.

Paul noticed the hesitation. "I'm sorry to be so impetuous. Are you already in a relationship?"

Callie shook herself. "Oh, no. Sorry." Then she allowed herself a smile. "I'd love to."

The little Italian restaurant Paul took her to was charming. It sat on the corner of the main street that passed the town square and a side road that went into a fashionable neighborhood with its tree-lined streets and stately colonial-style houses. She had driven up the street several times just to look at the expensive, well-kept homes.

The weather had cleared and the sun had appeared. Much to Callie's delight, Paul requested an outside table.

"You've been here before?" Callie asked.

"Often. It's not far from the *Gazette* so I usually walk. Gives me an excuse to eat more." He patted his stomach. "I think you'll love it. And we must start with the garlic knots."

"Anything Italian is right up my alley."

"How is the Italian food in Ohio?"

"Not bad but we don't have many of these cute little locally owned establishments. Mainly the chain restaurants when it comes to Italian. But the Buckeye State is famous for its chili dogs."

"Now there's a culinary delight! You'll have to take me there to try one."

Callie smiled. "I just might do that."

Looking out onto the street, she noticed a light blue convertible, its white top folded down, coming toward them. What caught her eye was the driver and his passenger, snuggled up like two teenagers on their first date. "There's Marcus Brennan and his wife. Do you know her name?"

"He introduced her to me once; let me think." He scratched his forehead, recollection dawning. "Dianne, he called her Dianne."

"Did she come to the track often?"

"Usually just when she was trying to get her husband to come home. It wasn't a happy place for her, as you probably guessed from what he said."

Callie watched them turn the corner and drive toward the upscale neighborhood. It appeared Dianne had found happiness now as she rested her head against her husband's shoulder.

Chapter 20

The next morning's routine went without any complications. Callie jogged Sunny around the track while Smithfield watched from the rail.

When she brought Sunny off the track, the trainer approached. "Haylie, how do you think Sunny is doing?"

"I think she's wonderful. She pays attention to me, not to everything else going on around us."

"That's pretty remarkable for such a young filly."

"You can say that again." Callie chuckled.

"I think it's time to step up the training. Let's start

introducing the pacing hobbles."

While Callie was in the tack room cleaning the harness, Smithfield returned with a set of hobbles. He proceeded to give Callie the instructions he wanted her to follow for their use.

"Hobbles help the horse learn to move laterally instead of diagonally," he explained. "When the left front moves forward, the hobbles bring the left hind forward at the same time."

Callie nodded. She had learned to use hobbles at her home, but she allowed Smithfield the chance to explain how the hobbles would be used to train Sunny to pace, and where to position them above the horse's knees and hocks.

When he was finished, he looked her in the eyes and brought up the previous day's memorial service. "I appreciate that you came to the service yesterday. I know you didn't know any of those horses or their humans."

"I'm a horsewoman. A bit of me died in that fire with the horses." Callie struggled to control the tears that wanted to spill down her cheeks.

She looked down and scrubbed the harness. "Stanley, can I ask you a question?"

"Ask away, young lady."

"I met a woman yesterday named Sarah Ferguson. Do you know her?"

"Yes. Very well. Everyone around here does. She has been involved with the harness racing at Liberty track for decades. One of the 'Old Timers,' so to speak." Smithfield shifted his weight to the other foot. "Why do you ask?"

"Did you know that she moved her horses out of Barn 7 the day before the fire?" She looked up from the harness and into his eyes.

"I didn't know at the time, but I did learn about that later. Lucky for her," he said while leaning against a saddle rack.

"She told me she moved them because she thought the barn was unsafe."

Smithfield snorted. "Nothing wrong with that barn, and she knew it."

"Do you think there was some other reason for her to move her horses?" Callie's senses were tingling with curiosity.

"Well, let's just say there was a rumor going around that Dr. Taylor was going to be drug-testing all the horses in Barn 7 the next day."

Callie straightened. "Are you saying that would be an issue for her?"

"I'm just saying it makes me wonder about Mrs. Ferguson's motives. She has been caught before. Claimed she was just using a topical ointment and didn't know it contained banned drugs. At another time she claimed the hemp bedding she was using was responsible for the CBD exposure by her horses."

"You don't believe her?" Callie's eyes narrowed.

Smithfield shrugged. "Who's to say."

"Now that we know the fire was caused by arson, do you have any idea who might be behind it?" Callie asked, deciding to move forward boldly.

Smithfield folded his arms across his chest, let out a long breath of air through his mouth, and didn't immediately respond. Finally, he spoke. "There are so many rumors flying around. I don't know what to believe. The police have questioned everyone at the track. No one claims to know anything." He ran his fingers through his hair. "Of course, *someone* does, we just don't know if that someone is one of us!"

Callie wondered if she should share any of this with Paul, and if so, how much.

Chapter 21

The heavy summer air fell like a blanket over Callie's shoulders as she finished her morning chores—mucking stalls, feeding and watering the horses, cleaning harnesses. As she worked, her mind reviewed the list she had made the night before. A list of facts learned and questions unanswered.

Tommy Valdez is obviously in debt to Joey Castellano. For how much? How does he intend to repay him? Would an insurance claim on Eat My Dust solve his problem? Is that motive to start the fire? Is there any truth to Paul's suspicion that the horse was injured?

Sarah Ferguson fortunately (or conveniently) moved

her horses the day before the fire. Was she really concerned about the safety of Barn 7 or was Stanley right in suspecting she was avoiding a vet exam? If so, would she have a reason to start the fire? Where was she that night?

Marcus Brennan was losing his wife over his deep involvement with his valuable horse, Thunder's Echo. Was he desperate enough to put an end to the horse as a way to win his wife back?

The night watchman, JT, certainly had the opportunity, but what was his motive? Did he have an axe to grind against one of the owners or trainers? Serious enough to risk losing his job?

Who else might have benefited from the fire?

She stabbed the ground with the manure fork in frustration at how little she had learned. She decided to report to Frank Morrison as he had asked her to do. Maybe he would have some ideas.

When she arrived at Morrison's office, his door was ajar. He was sitting at his desk, his back to her looking at the computer screen. On the screen were black and white images from the track's security cameras. She waited, silently watching as he scrolled through the tapes. She watched him pause briefly, when something caught his eye, before continuing on. Once he reached the end of the tapes, he pressed DELETE. He spun his chair around, only then noticing Callie standing there.

"Callie…er I mean Haylie! Good to see you. Have you been standing there long?" A friendly smile graced his face.

"No. Just arrived." She helped herself to a chair. "Do you have a few minutes to talk to me?"

"Just a few. I have another meeting with the insurance company this morning." His mouth dropped into a frown. "They can be such a bother." His face suddenly reddened. He backpedaled quickly. "Oh, I didn't mean you. I understand you need to get to the bottom of the fire. What can I help you with?"

"I noticed you were watching the security tapes," she began.

"Yes. I do that every day."

"Did you watch them the day of the fire?"

Morrison visibly tensed and the veins on the side of his neck twitched. "Er…no. What with all the confusion."

"Oh, of course. Are those tapes still available?"

"I'm afraid not. They were recorded over the next night."

"I see. That's a shame."

"Yes. Well, what can I help you with?"

She relayed to him the items on her list. Saying it out loud made her realize how sparse her findings truly were.

Morrison listened attentively, his face passive, giving no indication of his thoughts. When Callie finished, he cleared his throat and interlocked his hands on top of his desk. Leaning forward he said, "Well, that isn't much, but you do have good instincts, that's for sure."

"Instincts haven't gotten me very far in this case."

"Oh, don't be discouraged. You'll find more. Just keep your eyes and ears open. But from what you are telling me, you really believe it's one of us that did it? I'm more inclined to think it was some homeless person wandering into the barn for a night of shelter. Maybe accidentally started some hay on fire while smoking."

Callie shook her head. "The investigators have determined that an accelerant was used. The fire was purposely set." The thought crossed Callie's mind that Morrison must surely know this. And if so, why try to redirect her?

Morrison pushed back in his chair. "Well, if, and that is a big *if,* let me just say, I think Marcus Brennan is a dead end. He loved that horse too much to want to kill him. He'd sell him before he'd do such a thing. Now Tommy Valdez and Sarah Ferguson might be worth looking into."

"What about the night watchman?"

"The police went over him pretty hard. The guy even had to take a polygraph."

"Did he pass?"

"Apparently he did."

"Then where should I focus my search? I'd appreciate anything you can give me."

Morrison leaned forward and rested his chin on his hand. His mouth twisted in concentration. Finally, lowering his hand and looking her in the eyes, he said, "As I said, Tommy Valdez and Sarah Ferguson would be where *I* would start."

Chapter 22

Hey, Haylie! I've been looking all over for you." Paul jogged to catch up to Callie as she left Morrison's office.

Callie stopped and turned, smiling. "I've been talking to Frank Morrison. What did you need?"

"I need some food! Want to join me?" His expression mixed excitement and pleading.

To Callie, Paul was a breath of fresh air, a moment of respite from the pressure she was feeling to investigate this crime. "That sounds wonderful. I haven't eaten for what feels like days!"

At a window table in a downtown Ashville cafe, Callie studied Paul as he looked over the menu. A stab of guilt at the deception she was carrying on hit her hard. He looked up, cocked his head. "What?"

Flustered, Callie shook her head and looked down. "Nothing."

"What were you thinking? Trying to decide between the BLT or the French Dip?"

Callie laughed. "No. I was just thinking how happy I am to have you for a friend."

He lowered the menu and reached for her hand. "I feel the same way. You are a breath of fresh air in an otherwise stuffy world."

Callie laughed again. "That's just what I was thinking about you! Say, Paul, do you remember when we first met, and you mentioned something about the possibility that Eat My Dust had been injured?"

"Yes. Have you heard anything?"

"No, I was hoping maybe you had."

"Not a word. That's a tight-lipped community that is." Paul rolled his eyes. "My editor has pointed out that I need to write another story about the fire. He said it's been too long between stories. But I'm at a loss. Have you learned anything I could follow up on?"

Knowing she was deceiving Paul, Callie nonetheless didn't share any of her meeting with Morrison.

As they ate their sandwiches, Callie chanced to glance out the window. Suddenly, her sandwich tasted like paste in her mouth. She started coughing.

"What is it?" Paul followed her gaze.

"Across the street. Isn't that Frank Morrison talking to Dianne Brennan?"

Paul peered more closely, squinting. "I can't really tell. My eyesight isn't that good."

"It is. I'm sure of it. And they seem to be having an

argument. I wonder what that's about."

"Hard to say. Maybe the Brennans owe for their board and don't want to pay, considering…"

"Yeah. Maybe." But Callie couldn't stop watching them. As the argument got more heated, Dianne shoved Morrison in the chest and stomped away. A short time later, she appeared in her light blue convertible driving past the restaurant. Morrison watched her go, a smile on his face.

A day after her lunch with Paul, Callie gathered several buckets and a scrub brush and took them out of the barn. She set them down by the water spigot and filled the first bucket with water. One by one she started scrubbing.

A few minutes into the job, she heard Tommy Valdez arguing with someone. "I told you I'd pay you as soon as I can collect on the insurance. I can't help it if they don't want to pay until the investigation is complete!"

"That's not my problem. My problem is YOU! I've been patient enough. Get me that money or there will be hell to pay!"

The shouting stopped. Joey Castellano stomped out of

the barn. Seeing Callie where she stood hunched over the buckets, he tipped his hat and walked to his car.

When she carried the clean buckets back into the barn, Valdez was standing in the middle of the aisle, his face red, his arms folded across his chest. His breaths came in short, loud bursts. Seeing her, he forced a smile.

"Haylie. How are you doing today?" His voice was a little too gruff.

"Fine, thank you. I'm almost done for the day."

"Good. That's good." He unfolded his arms and took a deep breath. "Say, I'm glad I ran into you." He walked up to her and relieved her of some of the buckets. "I was telling Sarah Ferguson what a great exercise driver you are, and she wondered if you could fit in helping her with some fillies she is bringing along."

Callie immediately realized this was her chance to learn more about Sarah Ferguson. "I'd be happy to."

"You'd need to go to her place. She has all her horses at home."

"I can do that."

"Stop by my office in Barn 6 and I'll give you her phone number and address."

"Great," Callie said. "And Mr. Valdez…"

"Tommy."

"Tommy. Thank you for recommending me."

"My pleasure. Just don't let it interfere with what you are doing for Stanley. He comes first. Understood?"

Callie grinned, her green eyes sparkling. "Understood."

Chapter 24

The next afternoon, Callie followed her GPS to the address Valdez had given her. When the app announced, "You have arrived," she looked to her right. Stone pillars marked the entrance, topped with elegant lanterns that hinted at the property's evening grandeur. She turned off the country road and drove between them onto a magnificent tree-lined avenue that stretched ahead like a grand processional. Ancient oaks and maples formed a natural cathedral overhead, their branches intertwining to create a dappled canopy that filtered the afternoon light into dancing patterns across the drive. The trees were perfectly spaced, clearly planted generations ago with an eye toward creating this breathtaking approach.

Horses grazed peacefully in the pastures on either side of the paved roadway. This was clearly a "spare-no-expense" operation. The main house gradually came into view around a sweeping bend—a stately Georgian manor that spoke of old money and careful stewardship. Its whitewashed brick facade was complemented by hunter green shutters and a slate roof that had weathered decades of Pennsylvania seasons. Mature boxwood hedges lined the circular drive that curved before the front entrance, while established gardens burst with seasonal blooms.

Beyond the main house, Callie caught sight of the crown jewel: an immaculate stable complex with a distinctive cupola topped by a weathervane of a harness racer. The barn's painted brick walls sparkled in traditional colors—bright white with green trim. Neat gravel paths connected various outbuildings, and she could see to one side, the geometric precision of an oval track with its perfectly maintained footing.

The entire scene exuded a timeless quality, as if this corner of Pennsylvania had been preserved as a testament to the art of horsemanship and the grace of country living.

During the entire drive to the Ferguson farm, Callie pondered why Morrison had felt Sarah Ferguson should be investigated. From what she was seeing before her, money was not an issue. She made a note to have her boss at Mutual Assurance send her the police report on the interview they conducted with Sarah Ferguson. Then again, perhaps Morrison was just bitter about her accusations of unsafe practices and facilities at Barn 7.

As per instructions, Callie turned left just before the mansion and headed toward the stables. She parked near the front door of the barn. Her old Honda stuck out like a donkey in a herd of thoroughbreds next to the Cadillac

Sarah drove.

Climbing out of her car, Callie paused long enough to tuck in her shirt and run her fingers through her hair. Lifting her chin, she walked through the open barn door like she belonged there. Then she froze.

The interior took her breath away—this wasn't just a barn, but a cathedral dedicated to equestrian excellence. Soaring timber beams arched overhead like the ribs of some magnificent beast, while clerestory windows above the two rows of stalls sent shafts of golden light cascading down the wide central aisle. The air carried the warm, earthy scent of hay mingled with leather oil and the faintest hint of lavender from sachets tucked discreetly along the stall doors.

Each stall was a masterpiece of craftsmanship, fitted with gleaming brass hardware and rich mahogany panels that had been polished to a mirror shine. Ornate nameplates bore elegant script identifying each resident: "Midnight's Promise," "Sterling Dawn," "Lady Arabesque." The horses within—all sleek and well-muscled—stood with the quiet dignity of royalty, their coats gleaming like silk in the filtered sunlight.

Hanging on the fronts of the stall doors were plaid baker blankets embroidered with the Ferguson family crest. Everything spoke of old money and older traditions.

At the far end, Callie glimpsed a heated wash bay tiled in cream marble, and beyond that, what appeared to be a trophy room whose walls glinted with ribbons and silver cups. This was a place where champions were made, where bloodlines worth fortunes lived in luxury that would shame most five-star hotels.

She had never seen anything like it.

A warm, welcoming voice shook Callie from her reverie. "Well, don't just stand there. Come on in." Standing in front of a stall halfway down the aisleway,

Sarah Ferguson was stroking the beautiful face of a chestnut-colored horse, its large brown eyes nearly closed as it relished the gentle touch.

"Oh. Sorry, Ms. Ferguson. I didn't see you there." Callie could feel her face flush, but she forced her feet to step forward. "I was quite taken in by the beauty of your stable."

Ferguson stopped stroking the horse and looked around. "I guess I'm just used to it. I don't really notice it anymore. I should, really."

"Yes, you should. It is quite spectacular."

"Thank you, my dear. But I can't take any credit. It is my parents' creation. I merely inherited it."

"But you have been a careful steward to take such good care of it," Callie said, now standing directly in front of Sarah Ferguson.

Ferguson placed a gloved hand on Callie's cheek and smiled. "How kind of you to say, Haylie. I can tell I'm going to love having you around."

Ferguson led her through the pristine barn, stopping at each stall. "This is Midnight's Promise—she's my best broodmare. And here's Sterling Dawn, just back from the trainer."

They moved to the indoor arena where a chestnut colt circled on a lunge line, his handler calling out commands.

"That's Carter Koll," Ferguson said. "My new trainer."

Koll glanced over, assessing Callie with a practiced eye. "You're the new exercise driver?"

"That's right. I'm Haylie Norr."

"Well let's see how you handle Gray Dawn tomorrow afternoon. She's got opinions about who drives her."

On the fourth or fifth day, late in the afternoon, Callie brought Dawn back to the barn after jogging her around the track. As she checked the filly over, she noticed a cut on the filly's front heel on the off side—a common injury caused by the hind hoof overreaching and clipping the front leg.

Callie knew just how to treat such wounds. She headed to the tack room where she had spotted a small refrigerator and a first aid kit on the day she'd been given the tour. Rummaging through the kit, she found Betadine to clean the wound and an antibiotic paste to apply afterward.

Crouching down, Callie soaked a cloth with Betadine and gently cleaned the cut. Dawn jerked her foot in response to the antiseptic's sting, but Callie held tightly and finished the job with minimal fuss.

As she returned the bottle and tube to the first aid kit, her eyes drifted to the small refrigerator. Curious, she reached down and opened the door. Inside were several bottles and vials arranged on the shelves—vaccines, injectable antibiotics, and eye medications lined the front. All typical equine supplies.

But tucked behind these legitimate medications was a brown paper bag.

Callie reached in and pulled out the bag. Her brow furrowed as she peered inside. Three containers stared back at her: sodium bicarbonate, sodium citrate and sodium acetate. Her stomach dropped. She recognized these immediately—the components used for a "milkshake."

The illegal cocktail typically combined sodium bicarbonate mixed with sugar and electrolytes. Sometimes sodium citrate or sodium acetate were also mixed in. These alkalinizing agents raise the pH in a horse's blood and muscles, reducing lactic acid buildup and delaying fatigue. A horse given this mixture can run longer and harder than nature intended.

In Pennsylvania these agents are banned.

Callie's frown deepened as she carefully placed the containers back in the bag, her mind racing with the implications of what she'd discovered.

"What are you doing there?"

Callie whirled around. Sarah Ferguson was standing in the doorway.

"Oh. Uh. Dawn clipped her heel. I was looking for some antiseptic ointment."

"Well, next time, tell me and I'll get it for you." Ferguson's expression was a mix of anger and suspicion.

Callie felt her face get hot. "Of course. I didn't mean to snoop."

Ferguson moved to the refrigerator. She opened the door and glanced inside before closing it again.

She turned back to face Haylie. "I hired you to be an exercise driver. Not a vet."

"I'm sorry. It won't happen again." Callie rushed out of the room to finish taking care of Dawn.

Chapter 25

Callie was so lost in thought that the first few rings barely registered. When her phone's insistent buzzing finally broke through, she fumbled for the dashboard button without taking her eyes off the road.

"Hello?" Her voice came out distracted, almost breathless.

"Haylie, it's Paul."

Callie's frown reversed itself. "Paul. It's good to hear from you."

"You have been a hard one to catch, lately."

"I've been spending my afternoons at Sarah Ferguson's farm."

"Awww. That explains it. How is it?"

"It is the most beautiful place I have ever seen. But…" she stopped in mid-sentence. *Should I tell Paul what I found?* she wondered. *He'll surely think it's worth a story.*

"But what?"

"Oh, nothing. I'll talk to you about it later."

"How about over dinner tonight?"

"That Italian restaurant?"

"Perfect. I'll pick you up at six."

"I'm in my car now. I'll just meet you there."

Callie pulled apart a garlic knot as she perused the menu. She was so hungry, everything sounded good. Looking over her menu toward Paul she said, "What are you having?"

"I'm in the mood for chicken parm. How about you?"

Setting her menu down, Callie said, "That sounds great, but I think I'll stick with the tortellini with alfredo sauce."

Orders placed and garlic knots consumed, Paul leaned forward. "Tell me about Ferguson Farm."

Callie took a deep breath. Still hesitant to share what she had found, she decided to talk about the farm itself. "Paul, I doubt you've ever seen any place so beautiful."

"How so?"

"The grounds are like a botanical garden. The home is stunning. But it's the stable that took my breath away." Paul listened as Callie described the home where the Standardbreds lived and worked—cathedral ceilings, chandeliers lighting the aisleway, large box stalls with brass appointments.

Between bites of tortellini, she told him about each lovely filly she was working with.

By the time dessert came, she was finally out of words. She blushed. "I'm sorry. I've been talking your ear off. What have *you* been doing this past week?"

"I'm still investigating the fire. Something just doesn't feel right."

"What do you mean?"

"You told me that Morrison said he was suspicious of Sarah Ferguson and Tommy Valdez."

"Yes."

"Have you found out anything about either one of them?"

Callie chewed on her lip, trying to decide what to share. She took a deep breath. "I don't think Sarah Ferguson is involved in the fire. I believe she moved her mares so Dr. Taylor wouldn't find drugs in their system."

"Drugs? What kind?"

Scrunching her face, she told him about the containers she found in the tack room's refrigerator.

"So, you don't believe her motive in moving the mares was to save her horses from the fire."

"No, I don't."

"Okay. That's interesting. What about Valdez?"

"Tommy is another story. I believe he is in financial trouble. I think he is in debt to Joey Castellano."

"How much in debt?"

"I don't know. I've just seen him arguing with the bookie several times. And he was the first one of the owners to contact Mutual Assurance about a payout on his policy."

"How do you know that?"

Callie's breath caught as the weight of her mistake settled over her. She had just revealed something "Haylie" couldn't possibly know. Her fingers found a strand of hair, twisting it nervously around her index finger as she scrambled for an explanation.

"I..I mean…" she cleared her throat, forcing her voice to steady. "I overheard him complaining to someone—said he'd put in his request on day one but still hadn't seen a dime." The lie tasted bitter, but it was better than the truth.

"Should I write up a story about what you found at the Ferguson farm?"

"Oh no. Please don't. She'll know right away that I'm the one who told you and I'll certainly lose my job."

"Okay," he said as his shoulders slumped. "I'll have to see if I can find another way to get at it myself."

Callie savored the last hour of dinner, reluctant to let the evening end. Each meeting with Paul revealed new depths—tonight it was his humorous stories about his college life. As he talked, Callie couldn't help but notice that those sparkling blue eyes were becoming dangerously familiar territory.

She finally reached her car a little after nine, the day's heat still radiating from the asphalt. The sun had surrendered to a full moon that cast everything in silver. Instead of heading home to her empty apartment, she decided to go to Liberty to check on Sunny. It was 9:30 when she pulled through the gates and entered the grounds. Driving past the grandstand, she noticed JT running up to her car, waving his hands.

She braked and lowered her window. "Hi JT."

"Oh!" He stepped back, squinting in her headlights. "Miss Norr--I didn't know that was you."

"I just came to check on Sunny. Dr. Taylor gave her vaccinations today and I wanted to make sure she didn't have any reactions."

"Oh, sure, sure. Go right ahead."

Suddenly, Callie was struck with a thought. "Do you know most of the cars that enter at night?"

"Most of them, yes," his weathered face creased into a smile. "The regulars—owners, trainers…you know."

"Do you keep a record of them?"

"If I'm in the office, and I can see the video stream, sure. But I do rounds every three hours, check the barns." He gestured toward the sprawling facility. "Plenty come and go while I'm walking around. Then I have to watch the camera feed for those."

Callie's pulse quickened "Can you check the recordings from previous nights?"

JT shook his head. "No. Mr. Morrison handles all that. He reviews the footage each morning, then wipes it clean. Says there's no point keeping the record if nothing's wrong."

"So, the night of the fire…you don't have a record of that?"

"No." He paused, glancing back toward the office. "Matter of fact, Mr. Morrison gave me a new driver for the system the very next day. Never even saw most of that night's recording myself."

Chapter 26

It was an uneventful drive back to Philly after Callie checked on Sunny. Her phone buzzed just as she crossed the threshold of her apartment, her keys still dangling from the lock. She glanced at the screen and felt her pulse quicken—Carson Schmidt. Setting her bag on the entry table, she answered before the second ring.

"Mr. Schmidt, hello. Any news for me?" She struggled to keep her voice steady, professional.

"I just got the final report from the state fire marshal." His tone was grave, deliberately measured.

Callie gripped the back of a chair. "And…?"

"They have determined that the fire was caused by a

homemade incendiary device." He paused. Callie heard the rustle of papers, the creak of his desk chair. "Okay, here it is. They found traces of plastic from both one of those white plastic grocery bags as well as the kind of plastic used to make milk jugs. There were also cotton fragments from what appears to be a sock. Gasoline was the accelerant that was used."

Callie's mind raced ahead, connecting dots. "Putting that all together, what have they concluded?"

"They believe the arsonist brought a milk jug full of gasoline into the barn by carrying it in a grocery bag—something innocuous, easy to conceal if anyone saw them. The sock was used as a slow burning wick, giving the person plenty of time to get out of the barn undetected." He cleared his throat. "The jug was placed beside a bale of straw that was positioned in front of Thunder's Echo's stall. Once the straw caught fire, it was all over."

Callie's stomach clutched, and she had to lean against the chair for support. In her mind, she could see it all unfold with horrifying clarity: the small flame crawling along the cotton fibers, the sudden whoosh as the gasoline ignited, the straw exploding into an inferno. The smoke filling the barn. The horses screaming—that terrible, primal sound horses make when they're truly terrified. Thunder's Echo thrashing against his stall door in a futile attempt to escape. All this played out in her mind in a matter of seconds.

Someone had planned this. Someone had walked into that barn with murder in their heart, had carefully positioned their homemade firebomb, had lit that wick and walked away knowing exactly what would happen.

Hot tears stung her eyes, blurring her vision. She fought them back, blinking hard, her jaw clenched so tight it ached.

"Callie? You still there?" Carson's voice pulled her

back.

"Yes," she managed, her voice barely above a whisper. "I'm here."

"Find that guy, Callie!" Carson Schmidt hung up.

Chapter 27

ASHVILLE GAZETTE-BREAKING NEWS

**CAUSE OF FIRE FOUND AT
LIBERTY RACETRACK**
By Paul Coffman

ASHVILLE, PA - The state fire marshal has issued a report regarding the cause of the tragic fire at Liberty Racetrack on July 6th. A homemade incendiary device filled with gasoline in a plastic milk jug...

Paul's cell phone buzzed. "Hey!"
"Paul, how could you put me in such a terrible position?" Callie's voice sounded as if she was on the

verge of tears.

"What do you mean?"

"The story about the milk jug. Everyone at the track will think I told you that."

"Why would they think that? It's public record and anyone can find it. And I didn't name anyone as my source other than those records." He paused. "Why would you think they could possibly suspect you?"

Callie rubbed her hand through her hair, realizing that, perhaps, she had over-reacted. "I guess you're right. I just don't want to lose my job and as the newbie I have to be careful what people think or say about me."

Haylie." Stanley Smithfield's voice echoed through the barn as he strode down the concrete aisleway toward where Callie was grooming Sunny in the cross-ties.

"Morning, Mr. Smithfield." Callie glanced up from where she was bent over, hoof pick in hand, cleaning straw and manure from Sunny's left front hoof. The chestnut filly shifted her weight; ears pricked forward at the trainer's approach.

"I'm glad I caught you before you took her out. I want to make some changes in Sunny's training program."

Callie gently lowered Sunny's hoof and stood, one hand pressed against the small of her back. Not yet thirty, she already felt the daily aches that came with barn work. "What kind of changes?" she asked.

Smithfield stepped closer, his calloused hand coming to rest on her shoulder. When their eyes met, his voice was steady and deliberate. "Do you have a current USTA driver's license and Pennsylvania license?"

"I do. My father said I should keep it current just in case…"

"Terrific. I want you to be her driver in the Maple Leaf Pace in a couple of weeks."

Callie's hoof pick clattered to the ground. The Maple Leaf Pace—the biggest race for two-year-old fillies in the region. "You want me to…drive? In a stakes race?" Her voice came out higher than intended. "Me? Really? Do you think we're ready?"

Smithfield chuckled. "Don't sell yourself short, kid. You and I both know you have the skills. You've got natural hands and timing most drivers would kill for." Smithfield's mouth quirked into a rare smile. "Besides, I've got Magic Marvel to prep for the same card, and I can't drive them both. The way Sunny's been responding to the training cart and the hobbles tells me she's ready for the next step. Can't keep her in kindergarten forever."

Heat flushed Callie's cheeks—equal parts excitement and terror. "When do we start?"

"Right now. The starting gate will be circling the track for training starting in about twenty minutes."

Twenty minutes later, Callie found herself seated in the narrow racing sulky, the lightweight cart barely wider than her hips. Her helmet felt snug, the protective goggles already fogging slightly in the morning humidity. She pressed her feet against the stirrup bars as she gripped the leather lines, feeling every subtle movement transmitted through Sunny's bit.

Smithfield handed her a whip. "Use the whip to gently tap the shafts, or the number pad, but never whip the horse. The whip is for communication, not punishment. She'll understand what you're asking."

Callie drove Sunny to the track. As Stanley had said, the track had the starting gate operating for training. It was moving slowly around the track, arms extended.

As they approached the starting gate for the first time, Sunny's stride shortened, her neck arching with nervous energy. The mechanical wings of the gate stretched across the track like some industrial bird of prey.

"Easy, girl," Callie murmured, her voice steady despite her heart hammering in her ears. She tapped the whip on the shaft and drove Sunny toward the gate. Sunny planted her feet twenty yards from the starting gate, ears pinned flat.

"Easy," Smithfield called from the rail. "Let her look at it."

Callie sat motionless in the sulky, letting the filly process the mechanical monster with its outstretched metal arms as it moved slowly away.

After five minutes, Sunny took one tentative step forward. Then another.

By the third day, Sunny followed the gate at a walk without balking. By day five, she maintained a steady pace behind it.

"Now we're ready," Smithfield said when Callie and Sunny came off the track, satisfaction in his voice.

At the end of the week, Smithfield added another layer to the training. "Now comes the real work," he announced. "Once the arms have moved out of the way, tap the shaft with the whip and ask her to move over to the inside rail as quickly as you can. During a real race, if other horses have beaten you there, be patient and move into any opening along the rail that appears. Then let her relax and get into a nice rhythm. Bide your time, stay alert, and wait for the seam. Then thread the needle. Racing's won in the stretch, not the first turn."

Callie absorbed all his wise counsel. She started to turn to leave, then stopped. Turning back, she said, "Stanley, there's something I have to tell you."

Smithfield cocked his head and raised his eyebrows. "And what might that be?"

Callie took a deep breath. *It's now or never,* she told

herself. "You know I told you I was licensed to drive?"

Smithfield nodded.

"Well. My license is…"

"Spit it out."

"My license is under the name of Callie Oaks."

"You want to explain that one?"

Callie lifted her shoulders. "Not yet. I'll tell you the whole story in the near future." She brushed an errant strand of hair out of her face. "Until I do, please keep using Haylie Norr as my name."

"I'll have to use Callie Oaks when I sign you up for the race."

Callie chewed her bottom lip for a moment. Then she said, "Do what you have to do."

After two weeks of successful morning workouts with Sunny, Callie's confidence was building. Entering her in the big race didn't seem like such a bad idea, after all. Stanley had let the name issue drop. He said nothing more about it. Callie realized she'd have to level with him sometime…just not yet.

Finished with chores and training, Callie drove away from the barns and past the grandstand on her way to the Ferguson Farm. A light blue convertible, its white top folded down, squealed around the corner and came to a screeching stop in front of the track office. Callie slammed on her brakes just in time to avoid a collision, her breath caught in her throat as she gripped the steering wheel.

She stopped her car to catch her breath. Through the windshield, she watched as Dianne Brennan burst from her car and stormed toward the office, her heels clicking like gunshots on the pavement. Callie crouched down in her seat as Marcus Brennan's wife flung open the door and disappeared inside.

Callie's hands trembled on the steering wheel as she

sat frozen in her idling car. The engine hummed as her mind raced. What could make Dianne Brennan display this level of rage?

She should drive away. Pretend she hadn't seen anything. But curiosity and an obligation to fulfill her assignment kept her rooted to the spot. She found herself holding her breath and watching the office door with the intensity of a hawk eyeing prey.

Suddenly, the door burst open. Dianne Brennan emerged first, her face flushed, followed closely by Morrison. He remained a few steps behind as she made her way to her car. She flung open the car door and retrieved a thick manila envelope from the passenger seat. With deliberate force, she pressed it against Morrison's chest. Her lips moved in what could only be venomous words, delivered through clenched teeth and eyes narrowed to slits.

Morrison's hands came up to clutch the envelope as Dianne spun away from him. She threw herself into the driver's seat, slammed the door with enough force to rock the convertible, and gunned the engine. Tires squealed as she tore through the entrance gates, leaving a cloud of dust and the acrid smell of burned rubber.

Morrison stood motionless, watching the blue convertible disappear down the road. When he finally turned back toward the office, his expression had shifted to one of smug satisfaction—until his gaze swept across the parking area and landed on Callie.

Their eyes met through her windshield. The envelope still clutched in his hands, Morrison's satisfied smile faltered, replaced by something Callie couldn't read.

Chapter 28

Callie's phone buzzed against the nightstand just as she pulled back the covers. She had already turned down Paul's dinner invitation—the disturbing events involving Frank Morrison and Dianne Brennan had left her emotionally drained, her mind still churning over everything that had happened and what that might mean.

Part of her hoped it might be Paul calling back, trying once more to coax her out of her solitude. Maybe he was just what she needed.

Picking up the phone she recognized the number. It wasn't Paul. It was Carson Schmidt, her boss at Mutual Assurance.

"Hi, Mr. Schmidt." She tried to keep the weariness from her voice.

"Callie, sorry to bother you this late. I've been drowning in paperwork from this fire situation all evening."

"I can imagine. I'm feeling the same way."

She could practically hear his knowing smile through the phone. "Though I suspect not everything about this assignment has been a complete disaster for you."

"No," she admitted, sinking onto the edge of her bed. "It's reminded me why I fell in love with horses in the first place."

"Good to hear. Listen, I got that police report on Sarah Ferguson you requested."

Callie straightened. "And?"

"There is nothing there—clean as a whistle. The police cleared her. They're certain she had nothing to do with the fire. She has an airtight alibi for that night. Out of town company or some such."

Callie nodded. "I've come to the same conclusion. She's got her problems, but arson doesn't appear to be one of them."

"Problems I should be concerned about?"

"Nothing that affects Mutual Assurance directly."

"Then spare me the details," Schmidt said with a dry chuckle. "I've got enough complications to deal with as it is."

"Actually, before you go," Callie interjected before he could hang up. "Could you look into the Brennans' financial situation?"

"You mean do a financial background check? What are you looking for?"

"I'm not entirely sure yet, but I'd be particularly interested to know if Dianne Brennan has made any large cash withdrawals recently."

Chapter 29

The summer air at Liberty Racetrack buzzed with anticipation as the Maple Leaf Pace drew near. The prestigious race for two-year-old fillies captured the imagination of every trainer, owner, and stable hand on the grounds. In the early mornings, steam rose from coffee cups as clusters of horsemen and women gathered near the rail, their conversations peppered with boasts and challenges about their entries' chances come Saturday.

Stanley Smithfield moved through these groups like a maestro conducting an orchestra of good-natured rivalry. His face creased into a grin as he needled first one owner, about his filly's tendency to drift wide on the turns.

Another driver was cautioned about his filly's slow starts. He even ribbed Sarah Ferguson about her horse's questionable breeding. The banter flowed as freely as the morning mist rolling across the track's infield.

But when the crowds dispersed and the barn fell quiet except for the gentle nickering of horses and the rustle of hay, Smithfield's demeanor shifted dramatically. His shoulders squared, his jaw tightened, and every action became purposeful and precise. The jovial instigator vanished, replaced by a trainer who understood that careers—and fortunes—hung in the balance of a two-minute race.

The barn door slammed open. Callie looked up from brushing Sunny to see Tommy Valdez striding down the aisle, his usually immaculate tie loosened, dark circles shadowing his eyes, his hands fisted.

"Smithfield!" His voice ricocheted off the concrete floor.

Stanley stepped out of Magic's stall, curry comb still in hand. "What's wrong, Tommy?"

"What's wrong? I'll tell you what's wrong. This is not just fun and games, Smithfield." Valdez's voice carried the weight of a man trying desperately to hold on. "I'm expecting you to earn your paycheck on Saturday, and a lot more. I need you to win. Big."

The playful confidence drained from Smithfield's face in an instant. He straightened, recognizing the gravity in his boss's tone. "I know, boss. Haylie and I have been pushing the fillies hard. They're responding well to the training. I have every confidence they'll be ready to race."

Valdez stepped closer. "Hard isn't enough. I mean it when I say I need you to win *big* on Saturday."

Smithfield's chest expanded as he drew himself up to his full height. "We're planning on it, boss. These fillies have heart."

The exchange might have continued, but Valdez seemed to notice Callie's presence for the first time. His eyes flicked toward her with the wariness of a man carrying secrets too heavy for one person to bear. Without another word, he turned and strode away, his footsteps gradually fading into the thick morning air.

Callie waited until she was certain Valdez had left the barn before approaching Smithfield. The trainer stood motionless, staring at the concrete floor as if it held the answers he was seeking.

"Stanley," she began carefully, "I couldn't help but notice…Tommy seems more stressed about this race than usual."

Smithfield's laugh held no humor. He removed his cap and ran his fingers through his thinning, graying hair. "Stressed doesn't begin to cover it."

"What's going on?"

For a long moment, the only sounds were the soft whoosh of horses breathing and the distant rumble of the track maintenance crew. Smithfield glanced toward the barn entrance, then moved closer to Callie, lowering his voice to barely above a whisper.

"Don't breathe a word of this, but Tommy's drowning in debt. The kind that keeps you awake at night, wondering if you'll see another sunrise…wondering if you even want to."

Callie's pulse quickened. Her suspicions crystallized like frost on a winter window. "Numbers Castellano?"

Smithfield's eyes darted around the barn to make sure no one was near. Then he gave an almost imperceptible nod. "Tommy thought he had the system figured out. He made some bets that looked sure to pay off big," He shook his head with the weariness of someone who'd witnessed too many good men make bad choices. "The house always wins, Haylie. Always."

Smithfield brushed invisible dust off his pant legs

with his cap before continuing. "He decided to syndicate Dusty and make some money by selling shares in the horse. Seemed like the perfect solution. That horse was worth a fortune in shares—enough to get Tommy clear of his debts and then some."

Callie felt the pieces of the puzzle shifting in her mind. "But then Dusty died in the fire."

Smithfield's expression darkened. "That wasn't the real problem, Haylie. Three days before the barn went up in flames, Dusty pulled up lame during a workout. Dr. Taylor's examination revealed a completely torn suspensory ligament." His voice dropped to a whisper. "Dusty was never going to race again. Only a few of us knew, and it was supposed to stay that way."

The revelation hit Callie like a physical blow. She steadied herself against a stall door, feeling the warm breath of a curious filly against her palm. "Tommy couldn't syndicate a permanently injured horse," she said.

"Not for racing, anyway. Maybe for breeding eventually, but that's a long-term game. Tommy needed…needs…money now—before Numbers decides to collect in ways that don't involve cash."

Callie's throat felt dry. She swallowed. The question formed slowly, carefully picking her words. "Stanley…do you think there's any possibility that Tommy might have…that the fire might be his causing? To…to collect insurance money?"

The shock in Smithfield's eyes was so genuine, so profound, that Callie almost stepped away from him. "Never. Don't even think it. He might have his weaknesses when it comes to gambling, but he loves the horses and would never do such a thing."

"Desperate people…"

Smithfield shook his head. "Doesn't matter. I don't care how desperate he is." Smithfield's hand clenched into fists at his sides. "Tommy Valdez has spent his entire life around horses. He's watched foals take their first steps, nursed sick mares back to health, celebrated victories and mourned defeat. Whatever his flaws—and we all know gambling is a big one—he would never, *ever* harm a horse. Not for money, not for anything."

Callie studied Smithfield's face, searching for any crack in his certainty. She found none, only the fierce loyalty of a man defending someone he'd worked alongside for an entire year.

"People can surprise you when they're backed into a corner," she said quietly.

Smithfield shook his head with the finality of a judge's gavel. "Not Tommy. Not like that."

But as Callie walked away from the barn, the late summer breeze carrying the scent of hay and horse sweat, she couldn't shake the feeling that even the most loyal of men could be blind to uncomfortable truths. The thought of the story Paul would write if he knew what she had just learned sent shivers down her spine.

Chapter 30

The post assignments for the running of the Maple Leaf Pace had just been released when Smithfield came into the barn to find Callie. His boots scraped against the concrete aisle as he approached, and Callie looked up from checking Sunny's leg wraps. Her heart sank at the expression on his face.

"Post position eight." He pulled the assignment sheet from his jacket pocket and held it up. "Not what I was hoping for."

Callie's hands stilled on Sunny's cannon bone. She straightened slowly, the full weight of it settling over her shoulders. "Eight? We drew the outside?"

"'fraid so."

Callie cringed, turning to press her forehead against Sunny's warm neck. The outside position meant her filly had a longer race to run than the horses closer to the pilings that marked the inner track—an extra ten, maybe fifteen yards just to reach the first turn. Here she was, looking forward to her first big race with Sunny, the one they'd been training so hard for, and already the odds were stacked against them. She could picture it now: the gates swinging open, seven horses surging ahead while Sunny scrambled to find her stride on the outside, lost in the dust and the chaos.

Smithfield moved closer and punched her arm lightly, the gesture so familiar it almost made her smile. "Don't look so sad." His gruff voice softened. "You and Sunny make a great team. Your times have been better than the other horses in the field, even mine with Magic. You'll do fine."

"Fine." Callie echoed the word like it tasted bitter, still staring at the bay filly who'd turned her head to nuzzle Callie's shoulder, oblivious to the complication. "I didn't want just '*fine.*' I wanted a real shot at winning this."

Smithfield was quiet for a moment, and she could feel him studying her. Then he stepped around to face her, making her meet his eyes. "Listen to me. Remember what I told you when we started this whole thing—when you first climbed in the sulky and thought you could handle her?"

Callie nodded reluctantly.

"Same strategy applies here. You get to an opening on the rail as fast as possible. Don't panic about the outside draw. Use Sunny's speed once those gates swing shut and that car speeds away. Get her to the front if you can but find the rail before the first turn. After that, you wait for your chance to get around the horses and drivers in front of you." He paused, his eyes boring into hers. "You'll have to be patient. That's the hard part. But patience wins races, Haylie. Not the post position. Remember what I've told you a dozen times, racing's won in the stretch, not the first turn."

"But what if…"

"What if nothing." His voice was firm now, the voice of a driver who'd seen a hundred races and knew what he was talking about. "That filly trusts you. She'll race her heart out if you let her. The post position is just a number. What matters is what happens after the gates drive away." He reached out and gave Sunny's neck a solid pat. "And what happens is, you two are going to show everyone on that track what you're made of."

Callie drew in a long breath, feeling the knot in her stomach loosen slightly. Sunny pushed her nose into Callie's hands, snuffling for treats, and despite everything, Callie felt a smile tugging at her lips.

"You really think we can do this?"

Smithfield grinned. "I don't think, kid. I know. Now come on—we've got work to do. That rail position isn't going to find itself."

Chapter 31

Post Time for the Maple Leaf Pace was 7:00 p.m. Callie was grateful for the later time slot—the oppressive heat of the September day would have finally broken by then, leaving behind only the warm evening breeze that now stirred the flags atop the grandstand.

She guided Sunny onto the track with steady hands, her fingers light on the lines, and brought the filly to a halt with the gentlest of pressure.

The track announcer, introducing the entrants to the crowd, declared, "And in the eighth position…There's a Sunset, driven by Miss Haylie Oaks."

Callie wondered at the name the announcer used.

Haylie Oaks. How had Smithfield pulled that off?

She put her curiosity aside and waited, giving Sunny time to take it all in. The stadium lights blazed overhead, transforming the colorful sulkies into jewel-toned beacons that sparkled against the darkening sky. The drivers, resplendent in their multi-colored racing jumpsuits—electric blues, neon greens, brilliant crimsons—created an almost carnival-like spectacle. It was a far cry from the quiet morning training sessions she was used to. Callie was grateful Stanley had sent them out for a nighttime jog a few times. She sat up straighter, showing off her father's colors that she proudly wore.

Music blared over the loudspeakers, a pulsing rhythm that drowned out the excited chatter and occasional cheers from the crowd filling the stands. Callie could feel the energy radiating from the spectators as it vibrated through the warm evening air.

"This is it, Sunny," Callie whispered, leaning forward slightly so her voice would carry to her filly's alert ears. "We can do this. Just like we practiced."

Sunny's ears flicked back and forth, swiveling between Callie's voice and the commotion around them, as if she understood exactly what her driver had said. Callie felt a surge of affection for the young horse. They'd come so far together in such a short time.

Taking a steadying breath, Callie tapped the shaft lightly with her whip. Sunny stepped forward into a smooth jog, her muscles rippling beneath her sleek coat. As they warmed up, Sunny picked up speed and transitioned into her pacing gait, her legs moving in perfect lateral synchronization as they crossed in front of the grandstand. Callie could hear the announcer's voice booming over the speakers, though the words seemed distant. Suddenly, she heard someone calling her name.

"Haylie! Haylie!"

The voice cut through the noise of the crowd. She turned toward the grandstand and spotted Paul in the front row. He was standing, waving with both arms above his head like he was signaling a rescue plane.

Gathering the lines in one hand, she lifted the other in response. A grin spread across her face before she could stop it. The simple fact of being seen—of someone showing up just to watch her race—sent a warmth flooding through her body.

She faced forward again, her smile lingering as she tapped her whip against the shaft.

Reaching the end of the homestretch, Callie pulled on the left line, and Sunny responded immediately, turning smoothly around to head back toward the starting gate.

Eight horses with their sulkies and drivers lined up behind the mobile gates, the metal arms stretched out across the track. Callie maneuvered Sunny over toward post position eight—the far outside spot.

Callie looked over to post position four. Smithfield had Magic in place. Her trainer looked over at her and tapped his helmet with the end of his whip, flashing her an encouraging smile as he did so. Despite the knot of nerves in her stomach, Callie found herself smiling back. If he believed she was ready for this, then she had to put her trust in that and believe it too.

The starting car started moving down the track with all eight horses following in formation behind it, their drivers keeping careful watch on their positions. Callie kept her eyes focused over Sunny's croup, monitoring the filly's stride as they accelerated. In the car, the speedometer read fifteen miles per hour. Twenty. The wind whipped past Callie's face, making her eyes water slightly behind her goggles.

The moment they crossed the starting line everything exploded into motion. The metal arms swung forward with a whoosh, and the starting car accelerated sharply, veering right. In the same instant, all eight drivers directed their pacers to the left, each one fighting for position at the coveted rail.

Smithfield had Magic pacing spectacularly, her stride powerful and rhythmic, and the pair quickly claimed the lead position tight against the pylons that marked the inside track. Callie guided Sunny over with practiced hands, threading carefully through the chaos of horses and sulkies, and settled in against the pylons in the fourth-place position. Blood rushed in her ears, adrenaline singing through her veins. They were in a good spot—not leading, which would leave them vulnerable to being overtaken, but close enough to make a move when the opportunity presented itself.

Now came the hard part: patience. As Smithfield had drilled into her during countless training sessions, she had to wait for the right moment to advance. Unlike thoroughbred racing, where jockeys could sometimes squeeze through impossibly tight gaps, harness racing required space—enough room for the sulky's wheels to pass through without clipping another driver or horse and causing a collision. One wrong move could cause a catastrophic wreck.

Callie consciously relaxed her grip on the lines, letting Sunny settle into her rhythm. The filly's pacing stride lengthened and smoothed out, finding that sweet spot where power and efficiency merged. Through the lines, Callie could feel every movement of Sunny's body, the connection between them almost telepathic.

The hot, moist breath of a horse directly behind them washed over Callie's back—someone was following close, waiting for their own chance to advance. All around her, horses and drivers in various positions all jockeyed for advantage. A horse came up beside her on the outside, and Callie's stomach clenched as she realized she was boxed in—trapped with a horse in front, beside, and behind.

Don't panic. Be patient, be patient, she repeated to herself, forcing her breathing to remain steady. Smithfield's voice echoed in her memory: *Racing is ninety percent patience and ten percent knowing when to make your move.*

She stayed where she was all the way down the backstretch, Sunny maintaining her smooth, powerful pace. The position of the horses remained largely unchanged, everyone waiting, watching, calculating. Callie started to fear that an opening would never present itself, that she'd finish trapped in fourth place…or worse…never getting a chance to show what Sunny could really do.

But then, just as they entered the far turn, the horse to her side swung wide and broke stride—that telltale moment when a pacer's gait falls apart and they start galloping. The driver was required to immediately take his horse wide to the right, away from interfering with the other competitors while he worked to get his horse back into pace.

There it was—the perfect opportunity!

Callie's instincts kicked in. She tapped her whip on the shaft and pulled firmly on the right line, asking Sunny to move out and around the horse ahead of them. Sunny began to respond, her body shifting to the right—and then the line went completely slack in Callie's hand!

For one confused heartbeat, Callie stared at the strip of leather dangling loosely in her right hand, the other end flapping uselessly against Sunny's flank. The line had snapped!

Without the guiding pressure of the right line, Sunny didn't understand what was being asked of her. The confusing sensation of leather slapping against her side combined with Callie's unbalanced pull on the left line caused the filly to react instinctively. She turned sharply to the left, away from the perceived pressure, cutting between the pylons that bordered the trotting track.

"No, no, no—Sunny, whoa!" But Callie's voice was lost in the wind and the noise.

Everything happened with terrible, surreal clarity as one of the sulky's wheels clipped a pylon. Sunny was heading straight for the white metal railing that bordered the infield. Callie hauled back on the left line with both hands, but without the right line to balance the command, she had no way to steer, only to try to slow the panicked filly.

It wasn't enough.

Sunny hit the rail at an angle, her momentum carrying her up and over. Callie had a split second to register what was happening—the rail rising up to meet them, Sunny's haunches bunching as the filly tried desperately to clear the obstacle—and then she was airborne, the sulky lifting behind her as Sunny pulled it over the barrier. The world tilted. Callie felt herself leaving the sulky's set, still gripping the remaining line.

Behind her the hoofbeats thundered as the other horses raced past behind them. The crowd gasped. But Callie heard none of this as the sulky crashed down in the infield, Sunny stumbling to the turf.

Callie's last coherent thought before her head struck something solid was: *I'm sorry, Sunny.*

Then everything went dark.

Chapter 32

ASHVILLE GAZETTE

DRIVER INJURED IN SULKY ACCIDENT AT LIBERTY TRACK
By Paul Coffman

ASHVILLE, PA - A racing accident Saturday evening sent novice driver Haylie Norr Oaks to Mercy Hospital with head injuries when her two-year-old filly, There's a Sunset, bolted over the rail during the Maple Leaf Pace.

Track officials are investigating...

Paul stared at his screen, unable to write objectively about someone he was beginning to care so much about. His desk phone rang. "Where's my copy, Coffman?" his editor shouted through the phone. "This accident story should have been filed an hour ago."

Callie became aware of the world gradually—beeps first, steady and insistent, then the squeak of a cart's wheels rolling across linoleum, and finally the murmur of unfamiliar voices speaking in hushed tones just beyond her reach. Her eyelids weighed. She fought to open them.

When she finally succeeded, the world came into focus slowly. White ceiling tiles swam above her, slightly yellowed at the edges. Heavy curtains enclosed her bed on three sides, their institutional green fabric doing little to soften the clinical atmosphere. A monitor loomed beside her, its wires disappearing beneath the light blankets that covered her.

"Hello?" The word came out as barely more than a rasp. "Is anyone there?"

The curtain whipped open so quickly it rattled on its metal rings. Her mother rushed to her bedside, followed closely by her father. Behind them, Carson Schmidt hung back near the gap in the curtain, his usually composed face etched with worry, his hands deep in his pockets.

"Oh, Callie. We've been so worried about you." Her mother, Leti Oaks, bent over the bed rail and pressed her lips to Callie's forehead. Her hand smoothed the hair back from Callie's face with trembling fingers. "We've been so worried. *So* worried. We drove in from Ohio as soon as your boss called us."

"Sweetheart, do you remember what happened?" her father, Charles, said, moving to the opposite side of the bed. His large, calloused hand finding hers and squeezing gently. His eyes—usually so steady and sure—searched her face with barely concealed fear.

Callie lifted her free hand toward her head. One side was covered with a gauze bandage extending from her crown down past her left temple. "I…I…had an accident." The words came slowly.

"That's good. That's very good that you can remember." Her father's voice was carefully controlled, the tone he used when calming a spooking horse. He patted her arm. "Do you remember what caused it?"

Callie paused, her face twisted in confusion. She struggled to pull memories through the fog. "The line… the drive line. Something happened to the line—." Her eyes flew open, and she jerked upright so suddenly the monitor beside her started beeping frantically. "Sunny! Is Sunny okay?"

"Easy, easy." Both parents moved at once, their hands gentle but firm as they guided her back against the pillows. Her mother adjusted the blanket with fussy, nervous movements. "Don't upset yourself. She's going to be fine. The trainer told us she's a little banged up but nothing that won't heal."

Callie pressed her palms against her eyes, trying to block out the images flooding back—the leather line in her hand suddenly going slack, the confused and frightened horse heading for the rail, the world tilting and spinning. "The line broke. I couldn't stop her. She was so scared, and I couldn't stop her."

"Shh. It wasn't your fault." Her father's voice cracked slightly. "Accidents happen, sweetheart." He turned back to Schmidt. "Thank you for notifying us about the accident, Mr. Schmidt. We appreciate the courtesy."

Schmidt shifted his weight, looking decidedly uncomfortable. "I'm sorry to have to be the one to make the call. But given the circumstances—few people know her real situation."

"Is an undercover operation something you normally

do?" Callie's father asked, a twinge of anger in his voice. "And if so, why Callie? She can't be your most experienced investigator after all."

"Dad—" Callie started, but her father held up a hand.

"Not normally, Mr. Oaks," Schmidt said quietly. "Only in unusual circumstances such as this. We needed someone who could authentically integrate into the harness racing community, someone who could get close to the right people. We had no idea she'd end up actually racing."

"Then you don't know my daughter." Charles's jaw tightened. "You put Callie within a mile of a horse and a sulky, and there's no force on earth that'll keep her out of that seat. Perhaps you should have set some ground rules, some boundaries, before you sent her in blind."

As they continued their conversation about Callie's inability to resist anything involving horses, a knock sounded on the hospital room's door. Leti went to the door, grateful for the interruption. When she pulled the door open, she spoke briefly with someone in the hallway, then returned with a woman in her mid-forties wearing plain clothes but carrying herself with unmistakable authority.

"Callie, there's a police officer here," Leti said, her voice tight with fresh worry. "Do you feel up to talking with her?"

"A p-police officer? What for?" Callie knit her brows.

Rita Kowalski approached the bedside, her sensible shoes silent on the tile floor. She had kind eyes, Callie noticed, but they held something else too—a gravity that made Callie's insides twist. "Callie, I'm Detective Kowalski. I have been investigating the fire at the Liberty racetrack."

"Hello, Detective," Callie's brow furrowed, her gaze darting from the detective to her parents and back again.

"Callie, I need to tell you something, and I need you

to stay calm.”

The room went silent except for the persistent beeping of the monitor.

Kowalski pulled a large, plastic evidence bag from her satchel. Inside was a length of leather line, its end showing a clean cut three quarters of the way through leading to a ragged tear. “The drive line that broke,” she said, pulling it out of the bag and holding it up. “We recovered it from the scene. Callie—” she paused, making sure she had the young woman’s full attention. “The line had been cut nearly through. Someone used a blade on it. They left enough intact that it would hold for a while but fail under stress.”

The words seemed to hang in the air, not quite making sense.

“What are you saying?” Callie whispered.

Kowalski’s expression was grim. “What I’m saying, Miss Oaks, is that this wasn’t an accident.”

Chapter 33

The doctors insisted on keeping Callie for one more night, despite her repeated assurances that she was fine. Between her parents' worried hovering and the doctors' concerns about possible delayed concussion symptoms, Callie didn't have much say in the matter. Outnumbered, she resigned herself to her fate: several more hours of listening to the rhythmic beep of the heart monitor, the shuffle of nurses' shoes in the hallway, and the muted conversations drifting in from the nurses' station.

The afternoon crawled by with agonizing slowness. Callie flipped through channels on the mounted television, finding nothing that could hold her attention until she chanced upon the local news. A brief story about the accident at Liberty Racetrack appeared across the screen. The image of Sunny bolting over the rail, pulling Callie and the sulky with her, caused her monitor to react wildly. The nurses came running.

"I'm fine," she assured them. "I just saw the film of my accident. It was upsetting."

"Let's change the channel." Her mother got out of the chair where she'd been reading and clicked the remote until she found a Hallmark movie.

But changing the channel didn't erase the image replaying in Callie's mind, especially the part where Sunny went down, tangled in the harness and shafts. Her stomach twisted with a mixture of fear and anger. Someone had tried to hurt her—or worse.

That evening, when her parents finally left to find some dinner—her mother reluctantly, but her father nearly dragging her out the door—the hospital settled into a quieter kind of stillness. Callie was just reaching for the television remote when she heard a soft tap on the door.

"Come in." She expected a nurse with another round of vitals to check.

Paul stepped through the doorway, pausing just inside the room. He held a modest bouquet of daisies in one hand, their cheerful yellow and white faces at odds with the tension visible in his shoulders. A crooked smile played at the corners of his mouth. "I think I have the wrong room. I was looking for Haylie Norr." His voice was carefully light. "They say the patient in here is a young woman named Callie Oaks."

Callie looked down at her hands, feeling heat creep up her neck and into her face. The thin hospital blanket suddenly felt heavy. She said nothing for a few minutes while Paul just stood there, his weight shifting slightly from foot to foot, watching her with an expression she couldn't quite read. His lips pressed into a thin line. His jaw tightened. His face reflected hurt mixed with confusion, maybe anger simmering underneath.

"No," she finally said, her voice barely above a whisper. "You have the right room…if you still want to visit me."

Paul stepped closer to her bed, setting the flowers on the rolling table beside her untouched dinner tray. Up close, she could see the fine lines of fatigue around his eyes, the tightness in his jaw. "You want to tell me what's going on?" His tone was measured, controlled—which somehow made it worse than if he'd been yelling.

"I'm sorry that I lied to you." Callie met his gaze, truly contrite. "I had a job to do, and I had to keep my identity a secret. It wasn't personal."

"Secret, even from me?" His voice cracked on the last word. "I thought we had something special going. I thought…" He stopped, running a hand through his hair then laughed, a short hollow sound.

"We did…do." She leaned forward despite the pull on the wires attached to the monitor. "That is *if* you are willing. My feelings for you were not a lie, Paul. That was the only real thing in all of this…that and my love of harness racing and the horses."

"How can I know when you're telling the truth?" Paul clenched his jaw, the veins on his forehead pulsing with barely contained emotion. "How can I believe anything you say when everything I thought I knew about you was a fabrication?"

"Not everything." The pain Callie was feeling caused her to look away. "Most things about me were true. Just my job at the track. Why I was really there." She turned back and looked into Paul's eyes. "I was sent undercover by my company. I work for Mutual Assurance as a Claims Investigator. Because the fire was originally of unknown origin, they wanted me to start working at the track to see what I could find out. Once it was confirmed that it was arson, they wanted me to find out who might have been involved, who had motive, who had opportunity."

"So, no one knew your real identity?" Paul's voice was flat now, carefully neutral. "I wondered why they called you Haylie Oaks during the race."

"No one…except Frank Morrison."

Paul's eyebrows shot up. "Morrison knew? The whole time?"

"He and my boss at Mutual Assurance arranged the whole thing. The fake identity, the chance to work with Tommy, everything. I was reporting to Morrison because he wanted to cooperate with the insurance investigation."

"So, everyone else—Tommy, Smithfield, Sarah Ferguson—they all think you're just a harness racing junky who wandered in off the street?"

"Well, not exactly. Morrison made introductions. Arranged for me to start working as a groom and exercise driver. And Stanley learned my real name when he went to register me for the race. My license is under 'Callie Oaks.' I don't know how he managed to use the name 'Haylie' when he signed me up for the race." She paused and pursed her lips, debating whether to share what else she'd learned.

Reading her expression, Paul said, "What? There's something else isn't there."

Callie's fingers twisted in the blanket. "There is something I learned from the police. The accident…my accident…it wasn't an accident at all. Someone cut the driving line. Partially severed it so it would fail during the race."

The color drained from Paul's face. "Oh my gosh, Hay…Callie." He sank into the chair beside her bed, suddenly looking older than his years. "Someone tried to kill you."

"Or hurt me badly enough to send a message."

"Sounds to me like someone knew what you were up to." Paul leaned forward, his elbows on his knees. The anger in his expression shifting now, morphing into something else—concern, maybe even fear. "Someone wanted you gone."

"But how?" Callie's voice rose with frustration. "Only Morrison knew, unless he told someone."

"Or unless *he's* the one who doesn't like you snooping around." Paul's words hung in the air between them, heavy with implication.

Callie's eyes widened as the thought took root. Her mind immediately jumped to Morrison's meetings with Dianne Brennan—those angry conversations on the street and in the parking lot. The way Morrison tensed when he saw her watching them. The old video from the night of the fire. The flash drive now missing and replaced with a new one.

She shook her head in shock. "I can't believe he would do such a thing."

"What have you learned about him in your investigation? Anything at all?"

"I saw him, twice, meeting with Dianne Brennan. Remember when we were at the café a few days after the memorial service? They looked like they were arguing on the sidewalk."

Paul's face darkened. "I remember. I didn't think anything untoward was going on."

"Right. Then I saw them together again coming out of the office at the track. She shoved a large envelope at him, practically throwing it into his chest. She looked angry, furious in fact. When she left, he turned and saw me watching them."

"But that doesn't mean any of this is connected to the fire," Paul said, scratching his chin.

A sharp knock at the door interrupted them. They both

froze and looked up.

"Ms. Oaks?" A nurse poked her head in, oblivious to the tension. "Just need to check your vitals again."

As the nurse bustled in with her blood pressure cuff and thermometer, Callie caught Paul's eye over the woman's shoulder.

His expression shifted again. The wounded look lingered in his eyes, but his mouth formed into a hard line and his stance widened, solid and immovable. When the nurse finally left, Paul moved closer to the bed. He reached out tentatively, his hand hovering near hers before finally covering it. His palm was warm and comforting.

"I'm still angry," he said quietly. "I'm angry that you lied to me. I'm angry that you didn't trust me enough to tell me the truth. But I'm also terrified that someone tried to hurt you. And if Morrison's involved…" he squeezed her hand gently. "We need to figure this out. Together. No more secrets."

"Thank you, Paul."

"But what a story," Paul added, his eyes twinkling.

"You can't write about this!"

"But I'm a reporter. I'd be fired if my editor learned I ignored a development like this."

"You wouldn't know about it if I hadn't told you. I can't be your source for anything regarding this story."

That caused Paul to stop and think. Finally, he said: "You're right. If I'm going to write about this, I have to get it myself, some other way."

Callie felt tears prick her eyes again, but this time she didn't fight them. "No more secrets," she whispered. "I promise."

"Good." Paul's smile returned, softer this time, more genuine. "Because I don't want to lose you now. Not to Morrison, or to whoever cut that line."

Callie relaxed back into the pillow. With Paul's hand

in hers, she allowed herself a moment to simply breathe. To feel grateful she was alive. That Sunny was alive. And to acknowledge that despite everything—the lies, the danger, the investigation—her feelings for Paul were the most honest thing she'd experienced in months.

"Thank you for the flowers," was all she needed to say.

Chapter 34

Early afternoon saw Callie and her parents checking out of the hospital. The doctors had cleared her for discharge, but not without stern warnings: she was to go straight home and do nothing but rest for the next forty-eight hours—minimum!

"Did you hear that, Callie?" her mother said, gripping her daughter's shoulder as she walked beside the nurse pushing Callie in the wheelchair. "Straight home and rest. No exceptions."

"I heard, Mom," Callie said as she rolled her eyes. The lingering headache and persistent dizziness made even mild rebellion feel exhausting. Her father met them at the entrance to the hospital in her parents' old Buick.

She climbed into the back seat, its worn upholstery familiar and oddly comforting, and she sighed as she settled against the window.

The engine coughed to life, and they merged into the Philadelphia area traffic.

On the way home, Callie's father sat stoically behind the wheel, his eyes fixed on the road with the same quiet intensity he brought to everything. Callie knew he hated the city traffic, much preferring to sit in a sulky behind a horse and navigate the traffic on a racetrack.

Meanwhile, her mother twisted in the passenger seat so she could look back at Callie. She launched into a cheerful monologue. "Paul is such a nice young man. It is so kind of him to offer to sit with you so your father and I can head back home. I feel so much better knowing someone will be checking on you." She paused barely long enough to draw a breath. "Now, what did you say he does for a living? A newspaper man?"

"He is a sports reporter for the *Ashville Gazette*," Callie murmured, her gaze drifting across the passing city scape. But she wasn't really seeing the strip malls and traffic lights. Her mind had already returned to the track. To Sunny, undoubtedly recuperating in her stall.

"That's right. I remember now!" Her mother's voice pulled her back. "Your father and I saw his story about your accident after we got here. A sportswriter. How interesting. You know, your father and I stopped by your apartment this morning and filled your refrigerator. My goodness, Callie, it was practically empty. What on earth have you been eating?"

"Mom, I've been going back and forth between the track and Mrs. Ferguson's farm. I haven't exactly had time for grocery shopping."

Her mother clucked her tongue disapprovingly. "Well, you're stocked up now. We got milk, eggs, fresh vegetables, some of that soup you like…" And so it went, all the way back to Callie's apartment—a stream of maternal concern disguised as casual conversation, punctuated only by her father's occasional grunt of agreement.

When they pulled up to the modest brick building, Callie felt a wave of relief wash over her. Home. Then she spotted Paul's silver pickup truck parked out front, and despite everything—the disaster at the track, the concussion, the exhaustion—she felt herself smile.

Chapter 35

With hugs and kisses, and more than a few tears all around, Callie bid her parents goodbye as they set off to drive back to Ohio and the many responsibilities that awaited them there. She stood in the doorway, watching until their car disappeared around the corner, her hand raised in a final wave that no one could see anymore.

She shut the door and leaned against it for a moment, suddenly aware of the silence that had replaced her mother's fussing and her father's protective hovering. Then she turned to face Paul, who stood awkwardly in the center of her little living room, hands shoved in his pockets like a nervous teenager.

Her eyes scanned the room, and she couldn't help but notice that her mother had done far more than just stock the refrigerator. The entire space had been transformed—picked up, dusted, and vacuumed. Even the throw pillows on the couch were arranged with military precision. The coffee table gleamed. Paul's daisies sat in a vase of water in the center. Her stack of mail had been neatly sorted.

A smile tugged at Callie's lips, and a warm flood of affection washed through her at the thought of how much her parents loved her, how they showed it in these small, tangible ways.

Paul stepped forward, closing the distance between them and reaching out to take both her hands in his. The smile that Callie loved—the one that crinkled the corners of his eyes—appeared on his face and his expression softened. "Time for you to rest," he said gently, giving her hands a slight squeeze. "How about if I stay and watch a movie with you? Your choice. I'll even sit through one of those romantic comedies you love."

"That's a great idea, but I have to do something first."

His brow furrowed slightly. "What might that be?"

"I need to go to Liberty to check on Sunny. Will you take me?"

Paul's eyes widened and his smile dropped. "But the doctors and your parents gave you strict instructions to stay in bed and take it easy."

Callie looked around the room with exaggerated innocence, gesturing with one hand. "I don't see any doctors here. And my parents are on their way back to Ohio."

Paul let out a long, defeated sigh, tilting his head back. "You're going to get me in so much trouble."

Callie punched him gently on the arm, a playful glint in her eye. "I feel fine, Paul. Really. And we'll only stay for a few minutes, I promise. Just long enough to make sure Sunny's okay and hasn't been pining away for me."

Paul shook his head slowly, but she could see his resolve crumbling. "How can I possibly resist those puppy-dog eyes? Okay, but you have to promise me—and I mean really promise—that it will be just a few minutes. In and out."

Callie held up three fingers. "Scout's honor."

One of Paul's eyebrows rose skeptically. "Were you actually a scout?"

Callie's cheeks flushed pink as she dropped her hand. "Well…no. Not exactly. But I do keep my promises…" She paused, then added with a sheepish grin, "Usually."

Paul laughed despite himself, reaching for his car keys on the side table. "Usually. That's what worries me." But his eyes were warm with affection as he opened the door for her. "Come on, then. Let's go check on your horse before I come to my senses."

Chapter 36

The sun was low on the horizon, painting the sky in shades of amber and rose as they drove through the elegant, aging gates of Liberty Racetrack. Callie's fingers twisted nervously in her lap. She knew most of the trainers would have packed up and left by now—the evening feeding done, the horses settled for the night. She was glad of that since she didn't know what kind of reception she would face if she had to confront the backstretch community for the first time since her accident.

Did they know about her true identity? Would they accept her if they found out, or would they see her as just another outsider playing at being one of them? Or worse—might they see her as a traitor because she was working for the insurance company? She suddenly had second thoughts about coming at all, about walking back into this world that nearly killed her. But her concern for Sunny and the desire to check on her injuries overruled all other doubts.

"Paul." Callie touched his arm as he steered the pickup along the backstretch road toward Barn 6, where Sunny was stabled.

Paul turned his head and looked over at her, his eyes soft with understanding. "What is it?"

"Do the people at the track, other than Stanley and Morrison, know about my false identity?" The words tumbled out in a rush.

He shook his head. "I doubt it. None of the news stories about the accident referred to your real name. They kept calling you Haylie Oaks. As far as anyone knows, you're still Haylie, new driver for Tommy Valdez."

Callie let out a sigh of relief, feeling some of the tension drain from her shoulders. That persona had been kept safe for this long. Perhaps she could hold onto it a little longer.

Paul glanced over at her. "Does Smithfield know what you are really doing and who you work for?"

"Not yet. He just needed my real name for me to be able to drive."

"And he still put his trust in you?"

Callie smiled. "He didn't ask too many questions."

After a few minutes of silence, Callie asked, "Paul, you never told me who won The Maple Leaf Pace."

"Didn't you hear? Smithfield and Magic. They left everyone else far behind."

Callie sat back and smiled. Something good came out of that race after all.

As they pulled up to Barn 6, Callie noticed two figures

emerging from the barn door—Tommy Valdez and Joey Numbers Castellano. Walking in the opposite direction, heads bent close together, the two men did not notice her in the car. But Callie observed something unique in their interaction, something that made her go still. There was no threatening hostility being displayed between the two of them, no aggressive posturing, unlike every other encounter she had witnessed. On the contrary, they were laughing and talking excitedly. Tommy clapped Numbers on the shoulder like they were old friends sharing a private joke.

"That's odd," Callie said to Paul, unable to tear her eyes away from the retreating figures.

"What is?" Paul said as he turned off the truck and shoved his keys in his pocket.

"Maybe it's nothing." She hesitated, watching until the two men disappeared around the corner of Barn 5. "But I just noticed Tommy with Numbers and they seemed to be… happy. I've never seen that before. Those two have been at each other's throats since I got here."

She made a mental note to find out what had changed.

Callie pushed the door open as Paul climbed out and ran around the truck to help her. Extending his hand, he lifted her carefully out of the truck, supporting her weight as she found her footing. She smiled with gratitude. "You are very kind, but you don't have to worry so much about me."

"Oh yes, I do." His eyes held both humor and concern. "I don't trust you to take care of yourself! Someone has to keep you from climbing in a sulky the minute my back is turned."

He said it with a chuckle, but Callie heard the undercurrent of genuine worry beneath the teasing.

Arm in arm, they walked into the barn. The familiar smells washed over her—hay and leather, liniment and sweet feed, and the earthy musk of horses. The barn was quiet except for the occasional stomp of a hoof or the rustle of hay. They made their way down the center aisleway until they came to Sunny's stall.

The door stood open, and Stanley Smithfield was kneeling in the straw, his experienced hands working carefully over Sunny's knees, applying salve and wrapping bandages around her front legs.

Callie sucked in a quick breath. "Stanley, how is she doing?"

Smithfield started and looked up, his face registering surprise. "Haylie, you startled me."

Pleased that he called her by her undercover name without hesitation, Callie responded, "I'm so sorry! I didn't mean to scare you."

Smithfield stood up stiffly, brushing straw from his knees, and came to her. Without a word, he gathered her in a tight bear hug, his arms strong and protective around her. "You have scared me enough the last few days to last a lifetime," he murmured gruffly against her hair. Stepping back, he held her arms and looked her up and down with the assessing eye of someone who'd spent a lifetime evaluating the soundness of living creatures. "You look wonderful…considering. When did they let you out of the hospital?"

"Just today."

"Well, you wasted no time getting back here." There was approval in his voice, and something else— understanding, perhaps.

"I couldn't stay away. I needed to see Sunny. To see how she was doing." Callie's eyes were already drawn to the filly standing quietly in the center of the stall.

Smithfield turned back to the filly, his expression growing more serious. "Physically she'll be fine. The cuts and bruises will heal. Nothing's broken, thank goodness." He paused, choosing his words carefully. "Emotionally…I'm not so sure. I think we are going to have to start from ground zero with her training. She's spooked by everything now—the track, the rails, loud noises, sudden movements. She's remembering what happened, and horses don't forget fearful events easily."

Callie moved past him and went slowly up to the filly, speaking soft nonsense words. She threw her arms around Sunny's neck. Burying her face in the filly's mane, she breathed in deeply the healing scent of horse—the indefinable smell that spoke of belonging, of home.

Sunny turned her head and gave Callie a gentle nudge with her muzzle, blowing warm breath against her cheek in recognition.

"We'll heal together, my sweet Sunny," Callie whispered, her voice catching. "Both of us; I promise."

Behind her, she heard Paul and Smithfield speaking in low voices, but she didn't turn around. For this moment, there was only her and the filly, two souls bound together by trauma and survival, beginning the long road back to trust.

Chapter 37

A week later, Callie was given permission from the doctor to return to work at the track. The visit at the office had been brief but welcome—light duties only, no driving a sulky for at least another month, but she could begin working with the horses again, as long as she kept her feet on the ground. Callie had practically floated out of the medical building. Once in her car, she called her parents, her boss at Mutual Assurance and, of course, Paul, to tell them the good news.

Smithfield was visibly relieved to have her back. He had too many horses to train to do it all himself, and the temporary help he'd hired lacked Callie's intuitive touch with the horses. The moment she walked into the barn office, he'd grabbed his training schedule and started talking.

"Callie, I want you to work with Sunny first thing each day." Stanley's face reflected how tired he was, but his voice was gentle in a way that told her he understood what this meant to her. "This week, just take her for a walk around the track. Let her start getting used to the other harness racers as they jog past. She needs to build her confidence back gradually, and frankly, so do you."

Callie nodded, grateful he didn't sugarcoat it. They both knew what was at stake—not just Sunny's racing career, but Callie's own courage. She was eager to work with Sunny again to start their healing together.

The fall day hinted at the approaching winter—a crispness in the air that made her pull her barn jacket tighter, the brightly colored leaves floating through the air and fluttering down to the sandy track like confetti celebrating her return. The morning sun slanted low through the gaps in the grandstand, casting long shadows across the oval track. The familiar sounds enveloped her—the rhythmic thud of hooves, the jingle of harness hardware, trainers calling out instructions, the occasional whinny. There was nowhere she'd rather be.

But her assignment to do undercover investigation of the fire was never far from her mind. It had been almost four months now, and she still didn't know who was responsible. While her boss, Carson Schmidt, had tried to be patient, especially after her accident, the pressure from the insurance company was mounting. Her thoughts moved to the night she had come to the track and seen Tommy and Numbers being so uncharacteristically friendly to one another. The image had stayed with her, nagging at the edges of her consciousness. How could Tommy and Castellano have been walking companionably, laughing like old friends, when everyone knew they'd barely tolerated each other for years?

Once back in the barn with Sunny—who had been calm during their walk, startling only once when a tractor backfired—she searched the stalls for Stanley. The barn was quieter now, most of the horses out for their morning training. She passed one empty stall after another until she finally found him with Magic, brushing the filly's gleaming coat. She stopped at the stall door and leaned against the weathered wood.

"Say, Stanley, I forgot to congratulate you on your victory at the Maple Leaf Pace."

A wide grin filled Stanley's face, transforming it. He put an arm over Magic's neck with obvious affection. "She did an amazing job." Pride rang clear in his voice.

"Oh, Stanley, I'm so happy for you." And she meant it.

Stanley had been driving harness racers for decades and had done his best to pass his knowledge on to her in their training sessions. But even with all those years behind him, the thrill of winning never waned.

Stanley's smile disappeared as quickly as it had come. "We were in the lead the whole race. That's why I didn't know what happened to you and Sunny until after the race was over." He paused, his hand still on Magic's neck. "Truth be told, I'm glad I didn't see it. I saw the film and that was hard enough to watch."

"It was bad," Callie said simply. "But I'm moving on, Stanley."

"Of course you are. I wouldn't expect anything else." He resumed brushing Magic, though his movements were stiff. "You've got more grit than half the drivers here, male or female."

Callie absorbed the compliment hungrily, then carefully steered the conversation to a new topic. "Say, Stanley, remember last week when I came to visit Sunny on the day I was released from the hospital?"

"I sure do. I was mighty glad to see you up and about. You looked pale as a ghost, but you were standing, and that's what mattered."

"Well, as Paul was driving up to the barn, I happened to see Tommy and Numbers walking away from the barn together, and they seemed to be on friendly terms. Almost chummy, actually. What was that about?" She kept her tone casual, as though she was just mildly curious. But her investigator's instincts were on full alert.

Stanley's face cleared immediately, the mystery apparently no mystery at all. "I can tell you exactly what that was about. Between the winner's purse and his large bet on Magic—and I mean large—Tommy won so much money he was able to pay back his debt to Castellano in full. Handed it over in cash the next morning, from what I heard. He's been in a much better mood the last couple of weeks."

Callie felt something deflate inside her. Another dead end. "I'm glad to hear it. Do you think he'll learn his lesson? Stay away from gambling?"

Stanley snorted, a sound of such profound skepticism that it needed no translation. "I doubt it. Tommy's addicted to gambling. Sure wish he would, though. Man's going to end up in serious trouble one of these days, and a lucky win won't bail him out forever." He shook his head. "Some people got to learn the hard way, and some people never learn at all. Tommy's probably the second kind."

Callie nodded slowly, filing the information away even as disappointment settled in her chest. She'd been suspicious that Tommy was connected to the fire in order to pay his debts. But maybe she was seeing conspiracies where there were only the ordinary dramas of track life: debt, gambling, victory, and defeat.

As she walked back to Sunny's stall, she couldn't shake the feeling that she was missing something. The fire hadn't been an accident—the investigators had been certain of that. Someone had set it deliberately. And it was probably someone at this track. Two of her original suspects, Tommy Valdez and Sarah Ferguson, seemed to be in the clear. Where should she go from here?

She ran her hand along Sunny's neck, feeling the mare's warmth, her breathing steady. "Who did this, Sunny? Who killed those wonderful horses?" she whispered. "And why?"

Callie took a deep breath. She needed to get back to work. The investigation would continue, even if this particular lead had turned to dust. The truth was out there somewhere, hidden in the daily routines and casual conversations of track life.

She just had to keep looking.

Chapter 38

Carson Schmidt called her as she navigated the evening traffic toward home.

"Callie." His voice filled with fatigue. "Before your accident, you asked me to check into Dianne Brennan's finances. It took me a while to get permission from the police for a warrant to serve the bank, but I finally got it."

Callie gripped the steering wheel. She held her breath as she waited for him to continue.

"Over the last four months since the fire, Mrs. Brennan has withdrawn $5,000 every month. Like clockwork."

"Cash?" The word came out sharper than intended.

"Yes. Cash."

Callie's stomach tightened. "So, there's no way to trace where it went."

"That's right." Schmidt took a deep breath. "Look Callie, you realize it could mean nothing at all. I checked into her background. It turns out she has a disabled brother who needs round-the-clock care. She could simply be helping her parents with those expenses. Families do what they have to do."

"But were there any $5,000 withdrawals *before* the fire?" Callie changed lanes, her mind racing ahead.

A pause. "That's the suspicious part. No, there weren't. Not a single one in the previous twelve months I was able to review." Another pause. "Could just be a coincidence, though. The brother's condition might have deteriorated right around the same time."

Callie scrunched her face. "Maybe."

"Be careful with this, Callie. Twenty thousand dollars in cash withdrawals looks suspicious, I'll admit, but it's not proof of anything. We need a lot more information before we can tie this to the fire. We need to know what she did with that money."

Callie had an idea, but she wasn't ready to share it yet. "I know. Thanks for checking on that, Mr. Schmidt."

After they hung up, Callie drove the rest of the way home on autopilot, Schmidt's words echoing in her mind.

A hot shower did nothing to wash away her churning thoughts. As Callie stood before her closet, trying to decide what to wear for her dinner date with Paul, her mind kept circling back to Dianne Brennan.

Twenty thousand dollars. Four months. Always cash.

She pulled out a navy dress, then put it back, reaching instead for a cream-colored blouse and black slacks.

Was the attractive, petite woman she knew to be

Marcus Brennan's wife capable of being involved in the fire that killed her husband's stallion along with twenty-seven other horses? What could possibly be her motive?

And her interactions with Frank Morrison—the hushed conversations that abruptly ended with Dianne storming off—what did they mean?

Nothing about this made any sense at all. Nothing connected.

But twenty thousand dollars in untraceable cash, starting exactly when the fire happened? That wasn't nothing. That was something.

Callie finished dressing with mechanical efficiency, her reflection in the mirror showing a woman whose mind was clearly elsewhere. Paul would notice immediately. He had those skills every journalist seemed to possess. She'd have to try harder to be present tonight, to give him the attention he deserved.

But even as she applied her lipstick and grabbed her purse, Callie knew her thoughts would keep returning to Dianne Brennan and those cash withdrawals. To the question that now burned nearly as hot as the fire itself:

What was Dianne Brennan paying for?

Chapter 39

The little Italian restaurant on Main Street in Ashville had become their favorite meeting place. Table three, the one near the window overlooking the courthouse square, was now "their" table.

Callie spotted Paul through the glass before she pushed through the door, his shoulders hunched forward, fingers working at a garlic knot. Callie was immediately greeted by the heady aromas coming from the kitchen—oregano and roasted tomatoes and something yeasty that made her stomach growl with hunger. She checked her watch. Twenty minutes late.

"Sorry." She dropped her bag on the empty chair and

slid into her seat.

Paul stood halfway, gesturing at her chair, then settled back down. "Don't be." He smiled. "Just meant more knots for me." He pushed the basket toward her. Three left.

She took one. Tore it in half. The steam rose from the soft, white center.

"Hard first day back?"

Callie nodded, chewing. The garlic hit her tongue, followed by butter and salt. Perfect.

"Well." Paul set down his water glass. "Tell me about it. No more secrets, remember?"

"I remember."

She did. That night in the hospital when Paul confronted her about the undercover name she was using. It had now been a couple of weeks since she'd told him about the insurance investigation she was conducting, the inconsistencies, Tommy Valdez's gambling debts, Sarah Ferguson's horse drugging history, and the confrontation between Marcus Brennan's wife and Frank Morrison.

Callie leaned forward, dropping her voice. "You remember what I told you about Dianne Brennan and Frank Morrison?"

"Marcus Brennan's wife and the head of track security."

"Right." She glanced toward the kitchen, then back. "Carson Schmidt called me today. My boss at Mutual Assurance."

Paul waited.

"Dianne Brennan has been withdrawing five thousand dollars in cash every month since the fire."

Paul's hand holding the roll stopped halfway to his mouth. "Cash?"

"Cash."

"Four months. That's twenty grand."

"Twenty thousand dollars," Callie repeated. "From her personal account."

The waitress materialized beside their table, her auburn hair pulled back, her notepad ready. Paul barely looked up. "The usual for both of us, thanks."

"Cheese tortellini with alfredo for the lady, and chicken parmesan for the gentleman," the waitress said as she scribbled on her pad before leaving the table and disappearing into the kitchen.

Callie waited until the woman left. "Schmidt mentioned something about her brother. Medical care, he said."

"That's reasonable."

"Is it?"

Paul picked up his water glass again. Put it down without drinking. "You don't think so?"

"I keep seeing her in that parking lot at the track." Callie pulled apart another piece of garlic knot, not eating it. "The way she nearly threw that envelope at him. How angry her face looked as she was talking to him."

"You think she's paying him?"

Callie met his eyes. "I don't know what I think. But something doesn't feel right."

The dining room hummed around them—silverware on plates, conversations bleeding together, someone laughing too loud across the room. Through the window, the courthouse lights came on, yellow against the darkening sky.

"You told me Morrison reviewed the security footage from the night of the fire."

"Apparently, he always does."

"And? What was on the flash drive?"

"He replaced the flash drive the day after the fire. Gave the night watchman—JT—a new one. Said the old drive was corrupt or something."

Paul leaned back in his chair. "Where's the original drive now?"

"I don't know."

"Then it seems to me we need to find out."

Their salads arrived. Caesar for him, house for her. Callie picked up her fork but didn't eat. Her stomach had gone tight again, different from the hunger.

"How do we do that?"

Paul speared a crouton. Chewed. Swallowed. "We ask Morrison."

"Just like that?"

"Just like that." He smiled. "People can be terrible liars, especially when they're not expecting questions. We catch him off guard, see what he says. See what he doesn't say."

Callie pushed lettuce around her plate. "And if he's involved?"

"If he's involved, he'll make a mistake." Paul took another bite. "They always do."

She wanted to believe that. Wanted to believe the universe bent toward truth and justice, that secrets couldn't stay buried, that twenty thousand dollars in cash withdrawals would eventually tell their story.

But the several years she'd been investigating insurance fraud taught her to know better.

"Schmidt is getting impatient for me to end this investigation. He wants a report by next week," she said. "He's talking about denying all claims unless I can find out who is responsible."

"And who do you think is responsible?"

She finally ate a bite of salad. "I only have suspicions and suspicions aren't the proof I need."

"Then we'll just have to get proof."

Callie looked at him across the table—Paul with his training as a journalist. Paul, who listened when she needed to talk, who knew just which questions to ask.

"But won't that be a conflict with your job as a reporter?" she asked.

"Not if no one knows I'm doing it." He gave her that impish grin that she loved so much.

Paul was now offering to walk into the fire with her.

"Morrison arrives at the track by six every morning," Callie said, "and leaves around four in the afternoon. He usually stops at the Quick Mart on highway 422 on his way home for gas and a coffee."

Paul's eyebrows lifted. "You've been following him?"

"Before I started working at the Ferguson Farm in the afternoons, I usually drove home the same way at the same time. Since the accident, I haven't been going to help with Sarah's horses. But I'm guessing he's still following the same routine. I'll have to check."

The tortellini and chicken parmesan arrived. Callie looked down at the cheese-filled noodles swimming in alfredo sauce. Her appetite returned.

"Let's follow him one of these next few days," Paul said, cutting into his chicken. "We'll accidentally run into Morrison while we're getting gas. We'll ask him about the flash drive and security footage. See what happens."

Callie cut into a tortellini. The cheese stretched between her fork and the plate. "What if he doesn't talk?"

"Then we know that, too."

She ate. The pasta was perfect—hot, salty, the cheese melting against her tongue while her thoughts continued churning.

Twenty thousand dollars and a missing flash drive.

Were they even connected?

And Dianne Brennan, in her large house in Ashville, probably sitting down to her own dinner with her husband, probably not thinking about fires or insurance investigations, or the threats people make in parking lots. Or maybe that was just what she *was* thinking about.

Callie set down her fork.

"Paul?"

"Yeah?"

"If Morrison is involved…" She didn't finish.

He reached across the table. His hand covered hers. "Then we'll deal with it. Together."

She wanted to pull away. Wanted to tell him this was her investigation, her case, her risk to take alone. That he shouldn't risk compromising his status as a journalist.

But she didn't.

His hand stayed warm against hers until the waitress came back to refill their water, and even then, he was slow to let go.

Chapter 40

The next morning, Callie drove through the gates at the Liberty Racetrack at 6:00 a.m. The days were getting noticeably shorter, and dawn had not quite broken. The sky was caught between night and day—that flat, colorless hour when the track belonged only to trainers, grooms and their horses. As she drove past the grandstand on her way to the backstretch, her headlights swept across Frank Morrison's car already in its usual parking spot near the track office.

Her hands tightened on the wheel. Her heart pounded in her chest.

Soon. She would be confronting him soon. As soon

as she could build up the nerve.

The thought of Paul being there was the only thing keeping her steady.

Callie parked outside Barn 6 and killed the engine. The morning air hit her face, sharp and clean, and calmed her nerves somewhat. As she walked down the aisle toward Sunny's stall, she let the familiar equine perfume work its magic. She breathed in, letting the beloved scent of hay and horses ground her.

Her footsteps on the concrete aisle caught the attention of all the horses…especially Sunny. The filly was already waiting, her elegant head draped over the stall door, dark eyes soft with recognition. The filly nickered—a low, welcoming sound that never failed to spread the warmth of joy through Callie.

"Good morning, sweet girl." Callie pulled a carrot from her jacket pocket. Sunny's velvet lips brushed her palm as she took it, jaw working in methodical circles, crunching the treat with evident satisfaction.

Callie moved through her assigned chores with practiced efficiency. Feed bins were filled with grain. Water buckets sloshed as they were cleaned and refilled. The wheelbarrow's front wheel squeaked its familiar protest as she mucked out stalls, one after another, the rhythm of the work allowing her mind to settle.

By seven-thirty, the section of the barn assigned to Tommy Valdez's horses was in order. And thus went her routine for the first week back.

A few days later, after finishing her assigned chores in her section of the barn, Callie went into Sunny's stall and slipped the halter over the filly's muzzle. She buckled the throatlatch just snug enough that it wasn't too tight. She led her out onto the aisle and clipped the cross-ties on either side of the headstall, left side first, then right. Sunny stood square, patient, trusting.

Callie began grooming, starting with the rubber curry comb in small, firm circles over Sunny's sleek coat. The summer shine was fading now, the first dense fibers of winter growth beginning to push through. Sunny's eyelids drooped halfway, her lower lip going slack—the unmistakable look of a horse in complete contentment.

Callie switched to the body brush. She worked her way down the filly's neck, across her shoulders, over her back, and down each leg. She grabbed the hoof pick last and cleaned the sole of each hoof.

Just as she was about to take Sunny for her daily walk around the track, Stanley Smithfield's voice cut through the quiet barn.

"Haylie, I want to talk to you."

Callie set down the hoof pick and waited beside Sunny's shoulder as Smithfield approached, his gait unhurried, his expression thoughtful. He stopped a few feet away, hands resting on his hips, studying the filly with the appraising look Callie had come to recognize— the one that meant something was shifting.

"I have been thinking," the trainer said.

Callie nodded. This was how Smithfield operated— never impulsive, always deliberate. Decades of experience distilled into careful consideration before making a move.

"I know you were told to hold off driving for a while."

"The doctor's idea," Callie said. "Not mine!"

Smithfield smiled. "I've learned that about you." He paused, his gaze moving from Sunny to Callie. "Do you think you're ready now?"

Callie caught her breath. Excitement surged first, sharp and immediate, followed by a flutter of nervousness she couldn't quite suppress. She had felt perfectly fine for two weeks—no headaches, no dizzy spells, no lingering fog from the concussion. But getting back behind a horse, back in the sulky where everything could go sideways in a heartbeat—that was different.

"I...I think I'm just fine," she said carefully. "What do you have in mind?"

"I'd like to get Sunny back under harness and pulling a sulky. Then we'll move up to you driving again."

Callie reached out, rested one hand on Sunny's warm shoulder. "Well, I'm ready. Do you think she is?"

"There's only one way to find out."

Smithfield disappeared into the tack room and emerged carrying a harness draped over both arms—leather traces, back strap, breast collar, surcingle and pad. Piece by piece, the two of them put the harness on the filly. The breast collar went on first, then the saddle pad and surcingle, the breeching straps buckled and adjusted, the crupper fitted carefully beneath Sunny's tail. The filly stood motionless, ears flicking forward and back, tracking their movements but offering no resistance.

Finally, Smithfield lifted the racing bridle—blinders attached, check rein ready—and slipped it over Sunny's ears. Callie threaded the bit into place, gentle but firm, and buckled the throatlatch.

"Good girl," Callie murmured. "You remember this, don't you?"

Sunny's nostrils flared slightly, testing the air. She shifted her weight, felt the pressure of the harness settling across her back and chest. She gave Callie a gentle nudge with her muzzle as if to say, "Yes, I remember this, and it wasn't all good."

Together, Callie and Smithfield led her out of the barn, across the gap between buildings, and into the equipment shed where the sulkies were stored. Morning light slanted through the open door and illuminated the row of sulkies—racing carts, training carts, jog carts. Smithfield selected a light-weight training sulky, its seat worn smooth from years of use.

He rolled it out and positioned Sunny between the shafts. Callie stood at the filly's head, one hand on her cheek, stroking the soft space between her nostrils. She kept her voice low, steady, a continuous stream of reassurance.

"Easy now. Nothing to worry about. Just like before—before the accident."

Smithfield lifted the shafts slowly, bringing them up on either side of Sunny's barrel, and clipped them into the metal quick hitches on the sides of the surcingle. Metal clicked into place. The sulky settled into position behind her, its presence suddenly undeniable.

Sunny's head came up sharply. Her eyes widened.

Callie moved her hand to Sunny's neck. Keeping her voice calm, she said, "You're alright. You can do this."

For a long moment, Sunny trembled, muscles taut beneath her coat. Then, gradually, she exhaled. Her head lowered.

Smithfield stepped back, hands on hips, watching. "Well, that went well."

Callie pulled another piece of carrot from her pocket and offered it to Sunny, who took it delicately, shifting the bit in her mouth as she chewed the pieces of carrot. Callie looked into the filly's soft, brown eyes. "You're a wonderful, brave girl."

"That she is." Smithfield moved to the sulky, testing the shafts, checking the straps and quick hitches one last time. "Let's take her for a walk."

Callie attached a lead to Sunny's bit on the near side. Smithfield positioned himself near Sunny's head on the opposite side. Together, they started forward, taking slow, measured steps toward the shed door and the open track beyond.

Sunny hesitated for just a heartbeat, feeling the sulky's weight pulling gently behind her, then stepped forward.

One step. Then another.

The sulky rolled smoothly behind her, wheels turning without sound.

And just like that, they were moving.

Chapter 41

Paul's truck rolled to a stop beside Barn 6 at precisely 3:30 in the afternoon. Callie's call had come in that morning. Today was the day. She was ready to follow and approach Morrison. But the timing had to be exact. Catch Morrison too early and he'd still be buried in paperwork, too late and they'd miss him entirely.

He swung out of the cab and strode through the barn entrance. "Ca…I mean *Haylie*. I'm here."

Her face appeared above the half-door of the last stall, wisps of brown hair escaping from beneath a baseball cap. Callie balanced a manure fork piled high with soiled bedding. "Last one. Give me sixty seconds."

She dumped the load into a waiting wheelbarrow, then slid the stall door shut and latched it. Paul moved forward and gripped the handles before she could object.

"Where?"

"Dumpster out back. Just leave the wheelbarrow beside it." She swiped at her forehead with the back of her glove. "I'll grab my things."

In the tack room, Callie reached past hanging bridles, harnesses, and lead ropes to open her narrow locker. Her purse sat wedged between a spare jacket and her racing boots. As her fingers closed around the strap, her stomach tightened. It was time. Her boss wanted answers. She couldn't put it off any longer. They were really doing this—confronting Morrison about the missing flash drive, the one piece of evidence that might prove who was involved in setting the fire.

If he was involved, what then?

The question lodged in her throat. Morrison had access to everything at the track. The barns. The equipment. The surveillance system. If he'd orchestrated the fire, he could easily have sabotaged her sulky. The memory of the broken line flashed through her mind— the sickening moment when she lost control of her horse.

She pressed her palm against the cool metal of the locker. *Thank you, God, for Paul,* she said in a silent prayer. Whatever happened next, she wouldn't face it alone.

They crossed the packed dirt of the barn area to where Callie's Honda sat in the afternoon sun. Paul circled to the passenger side while Callie slid behind the wheel. She gripped it with both hands, staring through the windshield at the white siding on the barn, noticing a patch of peeling paint and a broken board.

Breathe. Just breathe.

Paul's hand settled on her forearm. "You okay?"

She exhaled slowly and turned. "Should we do this?"

"Why not?"

"Because if he's involved in the fire..." She paused, choosing her words. "If he cut that line on my sulky, if he's capable of that, then who knows what else he might do?"

"We talked about this." Paul's voice stayed level. "We need proof. The only way to get it is to push him, see how he reacts."

Callie nodded and turned the key. The engine caught and hummed. "We'll wait at the corner of the grandstand. Watch for him to leave."

She backed out and navigated the narrow road that connected the backside to the front of the facility—two different worlds, really. The barns smelled of hay and horses and honest sweat. The front was all polished glass and manicured landscaping, designed to impress the betting public.

Callie pulled over against the side wall of the grandstand and cut the engine. They climbed out and eased forward to the corner of the building where they had a clear view of the office entrance and the parking spaces reserved for track management.

Morrison's red Nissan sat in its designated spot, hood still cool in the shade of the building.

"Still here," Paul said.

Callie checked her watch. 4:05. "He usually leaves between four and four fifteen. Any minute now."

The waiting stretched. Somewhere in the maple trees lining the lot, a robin called and was answered. Traffic hummed on Route 422 beyond the trees. Callie shifted her weight from foot to foot. The plan had seemed solid last night. Now it felt flimsy, full of holes.

What if Morrison just refused to talk?

What if he saw through them immediately?

What if—

The office door swung open.

Frank Morrison emerged, briefcase in one hand, phone in the other. He paused on the steps to finish whatever conversation he was having, then pocketed the phone and headed for his car. No glance around. No hesitation. He moved like a man with nothing to hide.

The Nissan's engine roared—Morrison always revved it too high—and he swung out of the space in a tight arc.

"Let's go." Paul pulled her elbow.

They scrambled into the Honda. Callie started the engine, watching Morrison's taillights disappear through the front gates with their elegant sign: "Liberty Racetrack."

"Don't let him see you."

"I won't." Callie shifted into drive and rolled forward. "If he makes his usual stop, this'll work."

Route 422 stretched ahead, three lanes of late afternoon traffic heading east toward Philadelphia and its suburbs. Morrison's red Nissan was easy to spot six cars ahead, hugging the right lane and doing exactly sixty in a fifty-five zone. Always five over. Never more. The man drove like he managed everything else—by the rules, but with just enough bend to show he wasn't afraid of them.

Callie kept three cars between them, matching his speed. Her palms were damp on the steering wheel.

Seven miles out, Morrison's brake lights flared.

"Blinker's on," Paul said. "He's turning."

"Quick Mart." Callie exhaled. "Just like clockwork."

She signaled and slowed, pulling into the gas station just a minute behind Morrison. His Nissan sat at pump three, already connected and filling. Callie eased in behind him at pump two, her heart pounding so loudly she was sure it could be heard.

This was it.

She climbed out, hands steadier than she felt, and

swiped her card through the reader. The pump beeped its approval. She lifted the nozzle, inserted it in her tank, and squeezed the handle. The gas flowed while she searched for Morrison through her peripheral vision. He was nowhere to be seen. No doubt in the convenience store.

Callie kept her eyes on the digital numbers clicking higher on the pump display. Gallons. Dollars. Focus on something normal.

Morrison appeared from the store two minutes later, large coffee cup in hand, steam curling from the small opening in the lid. He moved toward his car.

Now.

"Callie?" His voice carried surprise, but not alarm.

She turned, letting her expression register recognition a half-second late. "Oh—Mr. Morrison. Hi."

"Heading home?"

"Yes. You too?"

"Every day, same routine." He lifted the coffee cup slightly. "Can't make the drive without it."

Callie pulled the nozzle from her tank and hung it up with a solid click. "Mr. Morrison, I'm so glad I ran into you. I've hit a wall with the fire investigation."

"Doesn't surprise me." Morrison sipped his coffee. "I told you from the start—nobody who works at my track would do something like that."

"I remember." Callie moved around to the side of her car, closing the distance between them by half. "That's why I was hoping I could look at the surveillance footage from that night. Maybe there's something there."

Morrison's posture shifted. Subtle. His shoulders drew back maybe an inch. "I erase those tapes after I review them. They get reused."

"Right. But JT mentioned you brought him a new flash drive the next day." Callie kept her voice light, conversational. "So, I thought maybe you still had the old one. Just sitting in a drawer somewhere."

"I..." Morrison's jaw tightened. "I don't think so. If I even kept it, I wouldn't know where to look. Probably tossed it."

"Probably?"

"It's been months, Callie." He shifted the coffee cup to his other hand. "I don't catalog every piece of office supply I throw away."

Callie nodded slowly. "I understand. I just thought I'd ask. Mr. Schmidt's getting impatient for answers."

"Then tell Schmidt to pay the claims and move on." Morrison's voice carried an edge now, the friendly track manager receding. "We'd all like to put this behind us."

"You're right." Callie opened her car door. "Enjoy your evening. I'll see you tomorrow."

Morrison's eyes shifted past her, landing on Paul for the first time. His expression flickered—surprise, then something harder to read.

"Paul. Didn't see you there." He raised the coffee cup in a mock toast. "Enjoyed your piece on the Maple Leaf Pace. Good publicity for the track." Glancing at Callie, his face reddened. Then he added, "Even bad events can be good news for us. Gets people's attention."

"Thanks, Mr. Morrison." Paul returned a slight wave. "See you at the next race."

Morrison climbed into his Nissan without another word. The engine gunned and he pulled away, merging into traffic without looking back.

Callie sat motionless, gripping the steering wheel. The breath she'd been holding escaped in a rush.

"How'd I do?" Callie clicked her seatbelt.

"Perfect. You were perfect."

"Didn't feel perfect." She turned the key and the Honda came to life. Checking her mirror, she eased back onto Route 422, letting two cars pass before pulling out. "What do you think?"

"He knows more than he's saying."

"How can you tell?"

Paul adjusted the passenger mirror, watching Morrison's Nissan disappear into the distance. "Body language. I've interviewed enough liars to recognize the tells. The way he shifted when you asked about the flash drive. The pause before he answered." He turned to face her. "That flash drive still exists. I'd stake my career on it."

Callie's hands tightened on the wheel. "So, what do we do?"

"We find it." Paul pulled out his phone and started typing notes. "Because Morrison just gave us something valuable."

"What's that?"

"Confirmation that we're on the right track." He glanced up. "People don't lie about things that don't matter."

Callie merged into the left lane, accelerating past a truck. Behind them, the sun was starting its descent toward the horizon, painting the sky in shades of amber and rose. Beautiful. Everything looked beautiful and normal and safe.

But underneath, something was very wrong.

And now Frank Morrison knew they were asking questions.

Chapter 42

The next morning arrived sharp and brittle, red maple leaves floating on the breeze, the sun casting long autumn shadows over the barn rows, the light slanting gold through the changing trees. It was the kind of October day that made you glad to be alive.

Stanley Smithfield stood in the paddock beside Sunny, the filly already hitched to the sulky. One weathered hand was resting on the filly's neck, while the other gestured toward the driver's seat.

Callie climbed into the seat and placed her feet in the stirrups. With one hand she leaned forward and gathered up the long driving lines connected to Sunny's bit.

"Okay. Just take it slow," he said, his voice carrying that careful steadiness trainers used with skittish colts and shaken riders. "Walk if you want. Do a short jog if you feel like it. Remember, I'll be watching from behind Magic."

He checked the leather lines again. Then checked them once more. Callie had lost count of how many times he'd run those straps through his experienced fingers, searching for weak points, frayed edges, anything that might give way under pressure. Something he must have been sorry he didn't do the day of her accident.

Sunny appeared calm. Relaxed, even. Her dark eyes soft, ears forward, weight shifting comfortably between her hooves.

More than Callie could say for herself.

This was the first time she'd sat in a sulky since the accident. The leather lines felt slick in her sweating palms despite the cool air that carried the warning feel of the coming winter. Her hair clung damp beneath her helmet. A bead of sweat traced the curve of her cheekbone, then her jaw. She reached up and wiped it away.

She'd always prided herself on courage. On the kind of iron-spined determination that got you through the hard things.

But this was different. This was testing reserves she wasn't sure she had left.

Smithfield held out the whip.

She stared at it. Such a simple thing. Fiberglass shaft, leather popper, worn grip. How many times had she held one just like it? Hundreds. Thousands, maybe.

"You got this, girl." Smithfield's voice was gentle. He patted her back twice, the way her father used to.

Callie forced her mouth into something resembling a smile. She took the whip. Tapped the shaft lightly. "Let's walk, Sunny."

The filly stepped forward. Confident. Purposeful.

But when they reached the track entrance, Sunny hesitated.

Callie felt it immediately—that slight resistance in the lines, the way the horse's stride shortened, became uncertain. The filly was looking for someone at her head. Someone to face the world alongside her, to tell her it was safe to step onto that wide expanse of harrowed dirt.

The same way Callie found herself looking for Paul. Wanting him beside her in this investigation. Wanting that steady presence that made the dangerous things feel manageable.

"It's okay, Sunny." She kept her voice low, soothing. "I'm back here with you. You can do this. *We* can do this."

Sunny's ears flicked backward, listening. Then forward again.

She took one tentative step onto the track. Then another.

Magic appeared beside them, Smithfield guiding the filly with practiced ease.

"Magic and I will be your support team," he called over, positioning himself along the outside rail.

They walked. Slow. Steady. Keeping to the outside of the oval, taking their time. Twenty minutes to cover a mile that horses usually ate up in two. But neither Callie nor Sunny were ready for speed. Not yet.

"You want to jog?" Smithfield's voice drifted across the space between sulkies.

Callie felt something shift in her chest. A flutter. Anticipation cutting through the fear.

"Sure."

She clucked softly. Sunny's ears pricked forward.

And they jogged.

By the end of the day, Callie's arms ached with that good, honest exhaustion that came from hard work. Her shoulders were tight. Her lower back reminded her she'd been out of a sulky for weeks. But underneath the fatigue was something else.

Satisfaction. Maybe even a thread of hope.

Sunny had done well. Better than well. The filly was coming back.

Callie walked across the gravel lot toward her Honda, already thinking about a hot shower and whether Paul had any ideas about how to proceed with their investigation. The sun was dropping low, painting long shadows across the vehicles and barn buildings.

That's when she noticed the white envelope.

Tucked under her windshield wiper. Crisp. Bright against the dust-coated glass.

She stepped up to her car, bent over, and pulled it free. Her undercover name—Haylie Norr—was typed on the front. Neat. Precise. The kind of careful anonymity that made her pulse kick up.

She slid her finger under the flap. Inside were two sheets of paper, folded together.

The message was typed as well:

To Miss Norr,

I am writing to tell you that your life is in danger. I have been hired to scare you away from the track in order to stop the investigation of the fire. I am the one who cut your line before the race. The person who hired me was hoping that would be enough to scare you away. Since it hasn't, he is insisting that I go to greater measures to stop you.

I write this as a warning. Please stop your investigation or you might be killed.

I don't know the name of the person who hired me, but I did take his picture. I am including it here.

The words blurred slightly. Callie's heart climbed to her throat. Nausea rolled through her.

She unfolded the second page.

A black and white photocopy stared back at her. Grainy. High contrast. But clear enough.

Clear enough that recognition hit like a fist to her stomach.

She knew that face.

JT Walters.

Mild-mannered, humble, kind JT.

The paper trembled in her hand.

Behind her, a truck engine turned over. Someone called out a goodbye across the paddock. Normal sounds. The ordinary rhythm of a training facility winding down for the evening.

But nothing felt ordinary anymore.

JT Walters had hired someone to cut her line. JT Walters wanted her investigation stopped. JT Walters was willing to escalate to killing.

Callie stood beside her car in the cooling October air, holding proof that one of Liberty Racetrack's most trusted employees was behind the fire and now he wanted her dead.

Callie tried to remember how to breathe.

Chapter 43

Callie collapsed against her car, her eyes scanning the parking lot, jerking from one car to the next, searching for movement, for someone watching.

She fumbled in her bag, her hands still trembling as she reached in for her cell phone. The phone slipped away once before she managed to pull it out. She could barely control her movements as she struggled to punch the numbers that would connect her to Paul.

One ring. Two.

"Hey, I was wondering when you were going to call."

"Paul…" Her voice came out strangled.

The shift in his tone was immediate. "Callie, what is

it? What's wrong?"

"Paul, come quick." She swallowed hard. "I need help."

"Where are you?"

"At the track."

"I'm out the door right now."

Callie ended the call and climbed into her car, punching the lock button the instant the door closed. The click of the mechanism brought only marginal comfort. Her hands wouldn't stop shaking. She gripped the steering wheel, knuckles white, taking deep breaths. In through the nose. Out through the mouth. Her gaze swept the parking lot in rhythmic intervals—left to right, mirrors, left to right again.

A truck rumbled by on the access road. A distant door slammed. The track was settling into evening.

Where is Paul? She thought over and over.

It didn't take him long. Paul's truck appeared within minutes, engine roaring as it swung around the side of the nearest barn. Tires squealed. He jerked to a stop beside her, leaving his truck running, driver's door ajar, as he jumped out.

Callie's hands fumbled with the lock. She stumbled out and his arms were already there, catching her as her knees gave way. The tears came then, hot and unchecked, soaking into his shoulder.

He held her tightly while she sobbed. "I've got you," he murmured. "You're safe now."

She shuddered against him, her breath coming in ragged gasps. Paul continued to hold her while the worst of it passed.

Finally getting control of her tears long enough to speak, she pulled back and said, "S-someone left me a letter."

She extracted it from her jacket pocket—the paper already wrinkled from handling—and pressed it into his hands. She sniffled as she watched him peruse the letter.

Paul's expression shifted as he read. His jaw tightened. His eyes widening with each sentence. When he turned to the second page, he went completely still, staring at the photograph in disbelief.

"That's JT."

Callie brushed a tear from her cheek and nodded.

"JT?" Paul looked up, disbelief written across his face. "I can't believe that."

"I know." Her voice cracked. "It doesn't make sense."

Paul folded the letter carefully. "Let's get out of here," He guided her to his truck, one hand at her elbow. "We need to talk this over."

Paul drove to the town square, navigating the familiar streets in silence. Callie stared out the window, watching storefronts blur past, her mind circling the same impossible questions. The sky deepened to twilight, streetlights flickering on in sequence as they passed.

He parked near the old courthouse and came around to open her door. The October air bit through her jacket. She buttoned it up to her collar, but the chill had already settled into her bones. Paul led her to a park bench beneath an oak tree that had given up most of its leaves. He sat beside her and draped his arm across her shoulders.

For a moment, neither of them spoke.

"Okay, Callie." Paul's voice was measured. "Let's think about this. I find it hard to believe that JT would hire someone to hurt you."

She turned to look at him.

"Even if he was that kind of person," Paul continued, "something like that would be expensive. Where would a night watchman get that kind of money?"

"I was thinking the same thing." Callie pulled her jacket tighter. "But that is clearly him in the picture." She exhaled slowly before speaking again. "What should we do?"

"I say we go visit him."

Her head jerked up. "Visit him? When?"

"Tonight." Paul's expression hardened. "He doesn't report to work at the track until nine from what I understand. So, let's find his address and go right now."

Callie's pulse quickened again. She had visited several people as an insurance investigator, but this was different. This was personal. "What if he's dangerous?"

"Then we'll be careful." Paul squeezed her shoulder. "But I'm not letting you sit with this all night. We need answers."

She met his gaze and found something there that steadied her—determination threaded with protective anger.

She nodded twice.

"Okay," she whispered. "Let's go."

Chapter 44

Finding JT's address was easy. All it took was a quick call to Callie's boss at Mutual Assurance. Within mere minutes, Carson Schmidt called back with the address. Callie didn't tell him about the letter—knew he'd be upset. She merely explained it was part of the investigation and thanked him.

JT lived in a small, clapboard house on the south side of Ashville. The streets were narrow, and the neighborhood had aged gracefully into working-class respectability. Each house along Coal Street sat on a tiny lot, their postage-stamp yards separated by chain-link fences and shared driveways. Cracked sidewalks bordered the street, their concrete split by decades of freeze and thaw. A few trees, now bare of leaves, decorated the minimal yards with skeletal branches. Dogs barked in invisible back yards.

JT's house was in the middle of the block, distinguished only by its neatly painted trim and the wide walkway that split the well-trimmed front lawn.

Paul pulled to the curb and turned off the engine. The tick of cooling metal filled the silence. Both Paul and Callie sat motionless, staring at the house, each waiting for the other to speak first. A boy on a skateboard whizzed by, his wheels clicking on the cracks, the sound fading as he disappeared around the corner.

Callie's fingers tightened around the letter in her lap. She had read it a dozen times since finding it tucked under her windshield wiper, and each reading made her stomach clench tighter. Callie took a breath and turned to Paul for reassurance. "What if he really did hire someone?"

Paul turned to face her. "Then we need to know. But my gut says this whole thing smells wrong."

"Your gut?"

"Ten years of reading people as a journalist." He gestured toward the house. "Look at that place. Everything about it says honest, hardworking man. Not someone who hires muscle to intimidate a young woman."

Callie took a breath, steadying herself. "Let's go."

They both got out of the truck, their doors closing with synchronized thuds. The crisp air smelled of wood smoke from someone's fireplace. They walked up the sidewalk and ascended three steps to the door. The steps were swept clean, not a leaf in sight.

Callie glanced over at Paul, searching his face for reassurance. He gave her a slight nod. She reached out her hand and rapped her knuckles on the wooden screen door.

A small dog with a high-pitched bark announced their arrival. Callie heard footsteps on wood floors accompanied by the shuffle of the dog's claws.

The door opened and there stood JT holding a well-groomed miniature poodle, a smile breaking across his face the moment he recognized them. The security guard looked different out of uniform—smaller somehow, more vulnerable in his cardigan sweater and reading glasses perched on his head.

"Miss Norr. What a pleasure." He pushed the screen open with his free hand. "I never expected you to come visiting." The poodle whimpered. "Hush now, Lacey. These are friends."

"I have come to discuss a very important matter with you," Callie said, her rehearsed greeting sounding stiff and unnatural.

JT's smile faltered only slightly. "Well, come in, come in. It gets cold around here when the sun goes down." He stepped back, still holding the squirming dog. "Don't mind Lacey. She thinks she's a Rottweiler."

Callie and Paul stepped into the modest but well-cared-for house. The living room was small but immaculate. Photographs in mismatched frames covered one wall. The television sitting in one corner played the evening news with the volume down. The smell of something baking drifted from the kitchen.

A short woman with a kind face and warm smile came in from the kitchen, wiping flour from her hands on her apron. Her smile widened at the appearance of unexpected guests.

"Laurel, this is Miss Norr from the track, and this is…" JT paused.

"Paul Coffman," Paul supplied, extending his hand.

"Paul Coffman," JT repeated. "My wife, Laurel."

Laurel's handshake was warm and flour-soft. After offering tea—insisting really—she disappeared back through the doorway. JT set Lacey down and the dog immediately commenced sniffing Paul's shoes.

"Please, sit." JT motioned toward the over-stuffed sofa.

Callie perched on the edge, too tense to relax. Paul sat back, his posture deliberately casual, but his eyes never stopped moving, registering each detail.

Laurel returned a short while later with three cups of tea on a tray, steam rising in delicate curls, and a plate of cookies, clearly homemade and still warm. She set everything on the coffee table, smiled at them all, and retreated to the kitchen claiming a pot on the stove that needed stirring. The sound of running water and the gentle clank of dishes followed.

JT settled into a worn recliner across from them, his hands patting his lap to beckon Lacey. The dog was soon nestled in his lap.

"So, tell me what this important matter is that brought you here." JT watched Callie while he took a sip of tea.

Paul pulled the letter from his pocket. Callie set down her cup and took it from him, opening it and smoothing out the creases. "JT, I found this letter on my windshield this afternoon as I was leaving to go home for the day."

JT cocked his head, his eyebrows raised. "A letter? On your windshield?"

Callie reached across the coffee table, extending the letter toward him. "I'd like you to read it."

The security guard took the letter, adjusted his glasses, and started reading. His eyes moved across the first few lines, his face neutral. But the further he read, the darker his expression became. His jaw tightened. His breathing grew shallow. He flipped to the second page, and when his eyes landed on the photograph, his face lit up in shock—mouth opening, eyes widening, the letter trembling in his hands.

"That's me!" He looked up, staring at the two of them

sitting across from him. His voice cracked on the last word.

Callie nodded, watching him carefully. Paul remained stoic, his face unreadable.

"This person is trying to claim that I hired him to scare you off?" His voice cracked with disbelief. He read the letter again, his lips moving slightly. Suddenly his confusion transformed into anger, his face flushing red. "Why would anyone try to blame me for such a thing?"

"That's why we're here," Paul said, calmly. "We want to hear your side of the story."

"My side?" JT's voice rose. "You can't possibly believe this!" He shook the letter at them. "I would never do such a thing!" JT's voice was getting angrier with each word. "I've worked at the track for twenty years. I've never—never—done anything to harm anyone, let alone threaten a young woman's life!"

Lacey started barking again, sensing her owner's distress, and jumped off his lap.

Laurel appeared in the doorway. "JT?" She crossed the room in three strides. "What's wrong?"

"Nothing, dear. It's fine." But his voice betrayed him.

Callie leaned forward, her hands clasped together. "JT, we don't believe for a minute that you hired the person who wrote this letter." She paused, letting that sink in, watched his face relax slightly. "Do you have any idea who might want to frame you?"

JT stared at the letter again, his hands still shaking, his brow furrowing deeply. Then something shifted—a thought clicking into place—and his expression changed in an instant. "Wait a minute." He stood abruptly. "I know where this picture came from. I'll be right back."

JT dashed out of the room, his footsteps quick on the stairs. The ceiling creaked above them as he moved around.

Paul and Callie waited silently, exchanging glances.

Callie picked up her tea with both hands to keep them still.

Laurel retreated toward the kitchen and hovered in the doorway, wringing her hands in her apron.

When JT returned, he was slightly breathless, and he had a glossy 8 x 10 picture in his hand. "This was taken at the staff Christmas party last year."

Callie took it from his extended hand and Paul leaned in close to look. There was JT, exactly as he appeared in the letter—the same angle, the same expression, even the same shirt and tie. But the rest of the picture had been cropped before it was included in the threatening letter. The full photograph told a different story entirely.

It was a group picture with a dozen men and women. Next to JT, with a cheery smile on his face, was Frank Morrison.

Callie sucked in a sharp breath. She looked up at JT, then at Paul, then back at the photograph. "Someone in this picture wanted to implicate you." She continued staring at the photograph, her mind racing.

"Who else was at the party?" Paul asked, taking the picture from Callie and examining it more closely.

"We all were," JT said, sinking back in his chair. "The whole staff. It was at the clubhouse at the track."

"Did anyone else have this picture?" Paul asked, still staring at the photo.

"Everyone. Frank gave a copy to everyone."

"So, anyone could be the person who cropped the

picture," Callie said.

"Yes, but why me? What did I ever do to deserve this?"

Laurel walked up to her husband and took his hand.

"You're convenient," Paul said flatly. "You're security. You have access to everything at the track. You were there when the fire started. You're the perfect fall guy."

The night watchman squeezed his wife's hand and looked in her concerned eyes.

Callie saw something crumble in his expression and her heart ached for him. "JT, this is serious. Someone nearly killed me by cutting the driving lines before the race. And now they are threatening to finish the job if I don't stop investigating the fire." She looked directly at JT. "I need you to help me."

"Anything. What do you need?"

"Paul and I need to get into Frank Morrison's office…tonight."

JT's eyes widened. "Wait—you're talking about breaking into his office? That's illegal. I could lose my job. I could lose my security license." He glanced at Paul. "And you—if your paper finds out you broke into someone's office, you're done. They'd fire you in a heartbeat."

Callie stepped closer. "I know what we're asking. But someone tried to kill me, JT. They're still out there, and they're threatening to finish it. If Morrison's involved, there might be something in his office that proves it."

"And if he's not involved?" JT pressed. "Then we've just committed a crime for nothing."

Paul crossed his arms. "I've thought about that. My editor would have my head if this went sideways. But I'm not asking you to do anything I'm not willing to risk myself. And Callie's right—someone's already shown they're willing to kill. If we don't move now, we might not get another chance.”

JT looked between them, jaw working. “And if we get caught?”

“We won’t,” Callie said, her chin lifting, her fists planted on her hips. “Not with you helping us.”

Chapter 46

JT Walters rolled into the track parking lot at exactly 9 p.m. There was only one other vehicle in the lot, a nondescript small pickup truck belonging to Paul Coffman, reporter for the *Ashville Gazette.*

Under the sodium vapor lights, Paul watched from inside the cramped cab as JT killed his engine. Beside him, Callie sat rigid, her breath fogging the windshield in short bursts. The silence between them felt heavy. Callie swallowed.

JT emerged, glanced their direction—a quick flick of his eyes, nothing more—then headed for the office door. Keys jingled. The door opened and closed. A minute later, light bloomed in the office, shining through the window in the door.

"He saw us. Knows we're here," Callie whispered.

"Good. He knows the plan."

Through the windshield, they watched JT reappear, his silhouette passing by the clubhouse, headed toward the barns. His nightly ritual. Ninety minutes, give or take.

Callie checked her watch. "JT should have turned off the cameras by now…if he remembered."

"He remembered. He has a stake in this, too."

Paul and Callie waited. Paul's fingers drummed the steering wheel. The parking lot remained empty. According to plan, they were to wait ten minutes before making their move. Callie must have checked her watch a dozen times in those long minutes.

Finally. Ten minutes passed. "Let's go," Paul said, opening his door. Callie followed him out of the truck, the October air biting her face. She scanned the parking lot one last time. Following Paul across the asphalt, she forced herself not to look up at the security cameras mounted along the eaves. The office door loomed ahead.

Once inside, she felt a wave of relief. The office was quiet, the only sound the buzz from the overhead fluorescent bulbs. The smell of stale coffee permeated the room. Computers sat on desks, dark and cold. The day's mail fanned across the receptionist's desk, waiting to be opened.

Callie led the way to Frank Morrison's office, tucked away at the end of the hall. Even knowing they were the only people in the office, she couldn't help being on edge, checking each room and around each corner.

Morrison's door waited at the end. "Frank Morrison – Chief of Security" was written in bold letters across the middle panel of the door.

She pulled the key JT had given her from her coat

pocket, inserted it in the lock, and turned. The tumblers fell into place, and the door came open. She looked back at Paul. "Are you ready for this?"

"Now's the time. Let's do it."

They stepped into the room, shut the door behind them, then flipped on the overhead light. The fluorescent ceiling fixture stuttered to life, washing everything in harsh white light.

The office was familiar, the same windowless room, the same harness racing photos on the walls—Morrison in his younger days leaning back in his sulky, his horse frozen in midstride, the same clutter on the desk and credenza, the same straight-backed wooden chair she had occupied when she first met with Morrison several months ago.

"Where do we begin?" she whispered, fearing that even the walls could hear her.

"You start with the desk. I'll check the filing cabinets."

Callie pulled open the top desk drawer. Pens, paper clips, a calculator. She closed it silently and tried the next. Her hands trembled as she shuffled through Morrison's papers—invoices, pay slips, reports, work schedules, all the mundane machinery of running security at a racetrack. She replaced everything exactly as she found it, conscious that one misplaced document could give them away.

Across the room, Paul crouched before the filing cabinet, his fingers walking through tabs. "Find anything?" Paul whispered as he opened the second drawer.

"Nothing of value. Just paper and routine office supplies."

In the back of the lowest drawer in the filing cabinet, Paul found it. He let out a sharp gasp.

Callie's head snapped up.

Paul was crouched at the bottom filing cabinet drawer, one hand reaching behind a cluster of overstuffed file folders. When he withdrew it, he held an unmarked manila envelope. No address. No stamp. No reason to exist except to hide something.

Paul opened the clutch and reached inside, his fingers connecting with a small object he immediately recognized as a flash drive. "Eureka! I may have struck gold!" He pulled the flash drive from the envelope.

"Let's check," Callie said. Taking the drive from Paul, she inserted it into Morrison's computer. The computer sprang to life with the words: PASSWORD REQUIRED.

"Dang." Callie sat back, frustration burning in her chest. "I should have thought of the fact that the computer would be password protected. I could have brought my laptop."

Paul grabbed the flash drive and shoved it in his pocket. "Let's take it to my house and check it there. We can be back before JT finishes his rounds."

They killed the lights. Locked the door. Moved through the dimly lit office like ghosts who had never been there.

Jumping in the truck, Paul turned the key in the ignition and sped off the track property with the speed of someone who knew exactly how guilty he looked. They wound through Ashville's empty streets until they reached Paul's house.

Callie felt a mixture of excitement and dread. "What if this is the right flash drive?"

"Then we've hit pay dirt."

"What if there's nothing to see?"

Paul's hands tightened on the steering wheel. "That could happen, but my gut tells me otherwise. I don't think he would have saved it unless he was protecting himself or…" he stopped in mid-sentence.

Callie looked over at him. "Or what?"

"Oh, nothing. Just a thought." He shook his head. "Let's see what's on this tape before we jump to any conclusions."

But Callie saw the way his jaw worked. He had an idea. Something he wasn't ready to say out loud.

Paul's house sat on a quiet street near the center of town, close to his work at the *Ashville Gazette*. Inside, the place had the cluttered efficiency of a newsroom transplanted into domestic space. Stacks of newspapers. File folders. A computer setup that would make a day trader jealous.

Once inside, they lost no time. Paul booted up his computer and inserted the flash drive.

With heads close together, they opened up the only file on the drive: Date: July 6, 2026.

The video player opened. Grainy black and white images appeared. The familiar layout of the track's front gate and parking lot visible from four different camera angles. They pressed fast forward and watched as JT arrived at the office. The time stamp read 9:00 p.m. At 9:02 he left to make his rounds. They sped through the next ninety minutes in ten, the camera focused on a parking lot empty of all cars except the one JT had arrived in. Nothing moved other than a stray cat on the hunt.

JT returned to the office at 10:30 p.m., unlocked the door and went into the office. He emerged again at 11:30, but this time was only gone until a little after midnight.

Then, at 12:07 am, a car could be seen drifting past the entrance gates, slowing down, then moving on until it was out of the camera's range.

It was at 12:30 that something startling happened.

A figure in dark clothing materialized, moving along the edge of the frame. The figure stayed in the shadows cast by the grandstand, moving in the direction of the barns. As it passed by an outdoor light, a flash of white was clearly visible. The person was carrying a white bag, the kind used for grocery shopping.

Callie gripped Paul's arm. "That bag." Her voice came out strangled. "The fire inspector said the arsonist probably brought a gallon of gasoline in a white, plastic bag. That's him. That's the arsonist!"

Her heartbeat kicked into overdrive, and beads of sweat appeared on her forehead. The air in the room had suddenly been sucked out.

Paul didn't respond. Tension filled the room as they kept their eyes glued to the screen.

Ten minutes later, the same person was caught on screen running across the parking lot. But this time, at the last second, the person turned. Looked back at the office door. Looked directly at the camera.

The image was grainy. Black and white. But clear enough. Not a man. A woman.

Callie gasped. She could barely speak the words.

"Dianne Brennan."

Paul sat back, his face pale. "Well," he said quietly. "That explains a lot."

Outside, a car drove past Paul's house, its headlights washing across the walls. For a moment, neither of them moved. Just sat there, staring at the frozen image of Dianne Brennan's face, caught in the act of burning down a barn and killing twenty-eight horses.

Callie's phone buzzed. Text from JT: *Just finished the rounds. Where are you? Did you find anything?*

She looked at Paul. "We need to get back."

"We need to call the police."

"With what? Illegally obtained evidence from an unauthorized search?" Callie shook her head. "This proves she did it. But it doesn't prove why. And it definitely tells us that Morrison knew about it."

Paul paused the video, Dianne's face frozen on the screen. "Why would she do this? Kill twenty-eight horses? Risk everything?"

Callie stared at the image. "I don't know. But there has to be a reason."

Paul pulled out his phone and started searching. "Dianne Brennan...Ashville..." His fingers moved quickly across the screen. After a few minutes, he stopped. "Oh, no."

"What?"

He turned his phone toward her. An obituary from three months before the fire. Not for Dianne—but a memorial notice she'd posted on Facebook.

"Today marks two weeks since we lost our little one. The grief is overwhelming. I don't know how to move forward. Marcus is never home. I feel so alone."

Paul kept scrolling. "There's more." He typed quickly, switching tabs. "Found a comment thread on a harness racing forum, about a month before the fire. He read aloud from the screen. "Anyone else's spouse spend more time at the barn than at home? I'm starting to think my husband loves his horse more than me. I've tried therapy. I've tried talking. Nothing works. I don't know what else to do."

Callie felt her throat tighten. "She lost a baby."

"And then lost her husband to Thunder's Echo." Paul set down his phone. "She was desperate, Callie. Probably not thinking clearly."

"That doesn't excuse what she did."

"No. but it explains it." He looked back at the frozen image on the screen. "And it shows why it was easy for Morrison to manipulate her."

"And maybe he wasn't the only one."

Paul ejected the flash drive and held it up to the light. Such a small thing. Such enormous weight.

"So, what do we do?" he said.

Callie stood, her legs unsteady. "We put it back exactly where we found it. And then we figure out why Frank Morrison has been sitting on evidence that could send this woman to prison."

She checked her watch. They had twenty minutes to get back to the track, replace the drive, and disappear before JT had to turn the surveillance cameras back on.

Paul grabbed his keys. "Let's move."

They ran for the truck.

Once the flash drive was safely in its hiding place, Paul turned to Callie. "You realize this puts me in quite a bind."

"How so?"

"I'm sitting on the story of the century, and I can't say a word to anyone without jeopardizing the entire case."

Callie leaned over and kissed Paul on the cheek. "I knew from the first day I met you that you were the honorable type."

“It gets hard being honorable with my editor breathing down my neck.”

Chapter 48

The call came mid-afternoon while Callie was mucking stalls. She pulled off one glove with her teeth and answered on the third ring. "Mr. Schmidt. What can I do for you?"

"It's what I can do for you." His voice carried a current of satisfaction.

Callie set down her manure fork and stepped out of the stall. "What's that? Did you find something to help my investigation?"

"I ran Dianne Brennan's bank accounts again. There is another five-thousand cash withdrawal."

Her pulse quickened. "When?"

"Today. Two hours ago."

The pieces shifted, locking into place.

Callie ended the call and immediately punched Paul's number at the newspaper. He answered on the first ring.

"Paul, she just withdrew another five thousand. Cash. This has to be connected to Frank Morrison. He knows she's the one who started the fire. I think he's blackmailing her. Bleeding her dry."

"If she withdrew the money today, maybe she's going to deliver it to Morrison right now. It's our chance to get the proof we need to take to the police."

"My thoughts exactly."

"I'm already walking out the door. I'll be there in five minutes."

Callie left her chores half-done, pulled the barn door shut, and jogged between the barns to get to the racetrack's grandstand. Her boots kicked up loose gravel. Just as she arrived, she saw Paul's truck coming down the service road toward her.

He pulled alongside a copse of trees and cut the engine. "I just drove past the front entrance and didn't see Morrison or Mrs. Brennan. But Morrison's car is still there."

"Let's wait. If my suspicions are correct, she'll be coming. Get out and we'll hide in that stand of trees over there." Callie led the way to a spot that offered a good view of the front of the grandstand.

Callie and Paul positioned themselves in the shadow of the trees and waited. The grandstand stood majestically across the narrow drive, its weathered concrete façade absorbing what little afternoon light filtered through the overcast sky.

Both were too nervous to carry on much of a conversation. Instead, they let the scolding birds do the talking for them. A squirrel darted across the hood of the truck, paused to assess them, then disappeared into the pile of fallen leaves. A strong gust of cold wind brought down the last of the few remaining red maple leaves, some landing on their heads and shoulders, others on the hood of the truck.

Callie checked her phone. It was nearing 4 o'clock, Morrison's quitting time, when a light blue convertible, top up, sped across the asphalt parking lot and screeched to a stop in front of the track office.

Callie's thumb punched the video recorder on her phone just as she poked her elbow into Paul's ribs.

The office door opened and Frank Morrison stepped out. He didn't approach the car—just stood leaning against the building, arms folded across his chest, staring. His expression carried the self-satisfied quality of a man holding all the cards—an unattractive smirk that made Callie's stomach turn.

Dianne Brennan climbed out of her car, leaving the engine running. Even from across the drive, Callie could read the fury in her posture—jaw clenched, shoulders rigid, eyebrows drawn into a severe line. In her right hand, she gripped a manila envelope.

She didn't walk to Morrison. She marched.

"There." Brennan thrust the envelope at him. "There is the last of the money. Five thousand dollars. I've now paid you the entire twenty-five thousand dollars. Now I'm done with you."

Morrison initially made no move to take it. He let her stand there, arm extended, holding it out like an offering she was desperate to be rid of.

Taking his own sweet time, he took the envelope. Opened it. Shuffled through the bills. "Good, it's all here."

"Of course it's all there," she spat. "I'll be leaving now." She turned away then paused and looked back at Morrison. "I never want to hear from or see you again."

"Not so fast." Morrison's voice, calm and

conversational, carried across the parking lot to where Callie and Paul crouched in the shadows, recording the entire exchange. "I've been reconsidering our arrangement. I have decided that twenty-five thousand isn't enough to buy my silence."

"What?" she screeched.

Brennan's head snapped left, then right, searching for onlookers. Finding no one in the area, she drew closer to Morrison and lowered her voice. From behind the shelter of the trees, Callie could no longer make out her words. But her body language screamed everything—the sharp gestures, the forward lean, the trembling tension in her shoulders.

Morrison placed a hand on her shoulder which she promptly swatted away.

He shrugged, unbothered. He started talking, loud enough again for Callie and Paul to hear. "Considering the full scope of the loss—the destroyed barn, twenty-eight valuable harness racers, the insurance implications—I think you need to double that figure. Call it the price of staying out of prison. Because prison is exactly where you'll end up if my surveillance footage finds its way to the right people."

Brennan's voice rose in anger and desperation "How do I even know you have a tape?"

"Oh, I have it, alright." Morrison's smile widened. "I'm keeping it somewhere safe."

Paul and Callie exchanged a glance. They knew exactly where that tape was hidden. They had successfully returned it to its hiding place in Morrison's filing cabinet just over sixteen hours ago.

Brennan's shoulders collapsed inward. Her chin dropped to her chest. When she spoke again, her voice had lost its edge, replaced by the flat tone of defeat.

"Alright. But I can't come up with twenty-five thousand all at once. I'll have to keep paying you five thousand a month. That's all I can manage."

"Of course." Morrison folded the envelope and tucked it in his jacket pocket. "I'm an understanding man."

She lifted her chin, summoning some final reserve of defiance. "But this is it. No more. Do you hear me?"

Morrison nodded, magnanimous. "I think five more months of additional payments will more than settle your debt to society. Or at least to me."

Callie stopped the recording and slunk deeper into the shelter of the trees. Cold swept through her veins and she shivered.

They had them.

Chapter 49

Callie and Paul crouched low and hurried back to his truck, their breath forming small clouds in the October air. Neither spoke until they were safely sealed inside the cab, engine running, headlights cutting through the gathering dusk.

"We have all the proof we need," Callie said, her voice shaking with nervous tension.

"It sure seems like it." Paul checked the rear-view mirror in hopes that no one was following them. Then checked again. No sign of Morrison.

They drove in silence past barns 4 and 5, the truck's tires humming over the asphalt. Callie pressed her palm against her jacket pocket, feeling the rectangular outline of her phone. The video was there, pixels arranging themselves into the proof they needed.

"I need to finish feeding and mucking stalls, but before I do, I'm going to call Rita Kowalski, the police investigator."

"I think that's a good idea. It's time to turn this over to the authorities." Paul pulled up to the barn and cut the engine. "I'll help you with the feeding."

Callie dug through her purse until she found the business card Kowalski had pressed into her hand weeks ago. She punched the numbers before she could second-guess herself.

The investigator picked up on the second ring. "Kowalski."

"Rita, it's Callie Oaks from Mutual Assurance."

"Oh, yes, Callie. The one who's working undercover at the track to investigate the fire."

"That's right," Callie said, watching Paul disappear into the feed room and return with a bucket of grain. "You told me to call you if I uncovered anything important." She swallowed. "Well, I have, and you are going to want to hear what I've got."

Rita Kowalski and a plain clothes policeman arrived at the track a short time later. They found Callie and Paul in Barn 6 finishing the chores. Kowalski entered the barn like the experienced horsewoman she was.

"Callie," Kowalski called out as soon as she entered the barn.

Callie stuck her head out of the feed room doorway and looked both ways down the center aisle. Relieved to see no one but Paul, she hustled over to the policewoman, her boots leaving wet prints from where she'd hosed down the concrete. "I should have told you to call me Haylie. Everyone here thinks that's my name."

Rita's expression shifted—a flicker of concern.

"Sorry. I hope I didn't blow your cover."

"It appears no one's around, so I think we're safe."

"What did you want to show me?"

Callie pulled her phone from her jacket pocket and opened the video app. "Paul and I recorded this just a short time ago. It's Frank Morrison, the head of security, talking with Dianne Brennan. She's married to one of the owners whose horse was killed in the fire." Extending the phone toward Rita she added, "I'll let you watch it and see for yourself."

Rita and her companion leaned in, heads close together over the small screen. The audio crackled through the tiny speaker—Morrison's voice, then Dianne's, then the conversation that revealed the blackmail payments being made.

The two police officers watched the video, the expressions on their faces changing from curiosity to concentration. Then to something harder. Rita's jaw tightened.

When the recording ended, Rita looked up. "It appears we have our arsonist." Her tone was measured, professional. "But we need that surveillance tape if we want to prove it in court. Physical evidence to corroborate what we're hearing here."

"Paul and I know just where it is."

Kowalski's eyebrows lifted a fraction. "Dare I ask how you came to have that information?"

Paul emerged from a stall, manure fork in his hand. "Maybe it would be best if you didn't ask."

The corner of Rita's mouth twitched—not quite a smile. "I'll do this by the book. I'll need your phone to take to the judge to get a search warrant." She handed the phone to her partner.

The next morning, while Callie sat in the sulky behind Sunny during the training session, two unmarked police cars pulled up to the office beneath the grandstand.

Rita Kowalski stepped out, search warrant folded in her jacket pocket. Two detectives flanked her, one on either side. They moved through the entrance with purpose, their footsteps echoing off the concrete walls. They didn't hesitate until they reached Morrison's office—entering without knocking.

"Mr. Morrison." Her voice was calm but carried the weight of authority. "I have a search warrant for your office."

Morrison shot to his feet, his chair rolling backward and hitting the credenza. "What's this all about?"

"We have reason to believe you have evidence regarding the fire at Barn 7."

His face flushed crimson. "I have no such thing." The words came out too fast. "I have cooperated completely with the police. You know everything I know."

"Apparently not everything." Rita's voice remained level, controlled. She crossed the office with purposeful steps, her heels clicking against the linoleum.

She approached the file cabinet, bent down, and opened the bottom drawer.

There, tucked in the back exactly where Paul and Callie told her it would be, was a manila envelope.

Rita straightened, the envelope in her hand. She opened the clasp, tilted it. A flash drive slid into her palm—small and black.

She turned to Morrison, holding up the drive between her thumb and forefinger. The fluorescent lights caught its surface.

"I think this will give us all the information we need."

Morrison's mouth opened. Closed. The color drained from his face, leaving him pale except for two spots of red high on his cheeks.

The two police officers escorted him out.

Chapter 50

Rita Kowalski found Callie in the barn washing down Sunny. The mare stood patiently in the cross-ties while Callie worked a sponge across her withers, soap sliding in white ribbons down her coat. Seeing her approach, Callie tossed the sponge into the bucket of soapy water, sending bubbles splashing over the side.

"We have Frank Morrison in custody."

The relief hit Callie like a wave. "Now what?"

"Now we need to pay a visit to Dianne Brennan."

"We?"

Rita stepped closer, her expression showing understanding. "Yes, I'd like to take you along. You will be less threatening than a badge and a uniform.”

Callie felt a shiver work its way through her. She nodded only once. “I need to finish here,” she said, motioning to the wet filly beside her.

“Of course.” Kowalski sat on a bench and set to work on her phone.

Callie rinsed Sunny and quickly ran the sweat scraper over the filly’s body. She unclipped Sunny from the ties and led her back to her stall. The horse nickered softly as Callie latched the door.

Callie rubbed Sunny’s face. “I’ll be back soon.” Then she followed Rita out to the unmarked sedan.

It was past noon when they drove down Main Street in Ashville. Rita turned left at the corner by Paul and Callie’s favorite restaurant—the one with the garlic knots they couldn’t stop eating. Once off Main Street, the storefronts quickly gave way to residential neighborhoods. Within minutes, they entered the quiet, prosperous neighborhood the Brennans called home.

Rita pulled up to the curb in front of a large, colonial. Two stories, traditional lines, black shutters framing every window. The flower gardens along the foundation were neatly trimmed and put to bed for the coming winter. The walkway up to the front door was brick, set in a herringbone pattern.

Rita pulled out her badge and lifted the brass door knocker, rapping twice.

A man’s voice crackled through the Ring doorbell’s speaker. “Yes?”

“Detective Kowalski, here. I’ve come to ask Mrs. Brennan a few questions.”

The door swung open. Marcus Brennan stood in the threshold.

Callie had not seen him since the memorial service at the horse cemetery. The change shocked her. His hair was showing signs of gray. His skin had gone sallow, almost waxy. Dark bags sagged beneath his eyes. He looked like a man who had aged ten years in four months.

"Dianne is not here at the moment." His voice was flat. "Can *I* help you with something?"

"I'm afraid not," Rita said. "I really need to speak to Dianne in person. Do you know when she'll be back?"

"I'm expecting her anytime. She said she had an errand to run, but that was several hours ago." He glanced past them toward the empty driveway. "I really thought she'd be home by now."

"Do you mind if we wait?"

Brennan hesitated, then stepped back. "Suit yourself." He motioned to his left. "You can wait in the living room."

Callie and Rita stepped into the expensively furnished space. A fireplace was centered on an interior wall, its mantel lined with candles. A grand piano held a place of honor just beyond, its polished surface reflecting the afternoon light filtering through the windows. Two cream-colored sofas faced each other across a low coffee table, each decorated with a cascade of pastel pillows—pink, yellow, baby blue.

Callie lowered herself onto the nearest sofa. Her gaze drifted to the walls. Framed photographs everywhere. Most featured the same subject: a dark brown colt hitched to a sulky, muscles gleaming, head high. In every image, Marcus Brennan stood at the horse's head, beaming. His face bright. His posture proud.

A far different man than the hollow shell standing before them now.

Callie realized this horse must have been Thunder's Echo. The horse who died in the fire.

Callie's nerves prickled and she felt tears burning the backs of her eyes. This was much harder than driving a pacer in a harness race. Give her a mobile gate and a field of competitors any day. This—sitting in a stranger's living room, waiting for what felt like an ambush—was hard to bear. Callie had to remind herself of Dianne Brennan's guilt.

"Can I get you something to drink?" Brennan asked, hovering near the doorway. "Coffee? Water?"

"We're fine, thank you," Rita said.

Silence settled. Brennan shifted his weight. "Is this about the track? Insurance paperwork or something?"

"Just need to speak to your wife." Rita's smile was pleasant, revealing nothing.

"But what—"

"It won't take long, Mr. Brennan."

He rubbed the back of his neck, glancing at his watch. "I can't imagine what's taking her so long."

Callie tried to focus on the photographs, the piano, anything but the weight of Brennan's stare.

Rita's cell phone buzzed. She glanced at the screen, her expression shifting. "Please excuse me. I need to take this." She stood and walked into the entryway, her voice dropping to a murmur.

Callie avoided looking at Brennan. She strained to catch Rita's words, but the detective kept her responses clipped. Unintelligible mumbles. A pause. Then: "Where?" Another pause. "When?" Then, "I'm on my way."

When the detective returned to the living room, her face carried a look of shock. Maybe something worse.

"Mr. Brennan," Rita said quietly, "I need you to come with me. There has been an accident."

Chapter 51

The climb up Valley View Drive was both steep and serpentine. Rita gripped the wheel, taking each hairpin turn faster than she should, the Crown Victoria's tires squealing against the asphalt. Callie braced herself against the passenger door. In the back seat, Brennan sat rigid, his fingers digging into the leather upholstery.

Heavy silence filled the car.

Rita's jaw was set, her eyes fixed on the road ahead. Only she knew where they were going and why. She wasn't talking.

Callie kept glancing back at Brennan. The look on his face reflected both confusion and fear—his lips pressed into a bloodless line, his eyes darting from window to window as if searching for answers in the blur of trees rushing past.

Then Callie saw them. Flashing police lights strobing through the bare branches of oaks up ahead.

Brennan saw them too. He lurched forward, clutching the back of Kowalski's seat. "What's happened?" His voice cracked. "Is this where you're taking us? Does this involve my wife?"

Rita slowed, pulling up beside one of the patrol cars. The cruiser's radio crackled with dispatcher codes. She killed the engine and turned halfway in her seat. "Your wife has been in an accident." She met his eyes. "I don't know anything more."

Brennan didn't wait. He burst from the car, leaving the door open, and ran to where a cluster of uniformed officers gathered at the road's edge. They stood in a tight semicircle, looking over a steep precipice. From down the hill, an ambulance wailed its approach, the siren growing louder with each switchback.

Brennan pushed between two officers and looked down.

Several yards beneath where he stood, a light blue convertible sat crushed against a copse of trees. The front end was accordion-folded, the windshield a spider's web of shattered safety glass. Three policemen had scrambled down the embankment and were working around the driver's side door, prying at the door with crowbars.

A guttural scream rose from deep within Brennan. The sound didn't seem human. "My wife. That's my wife's car."

One of the officers turned, removing his hat. "Sir." He stepped closer. "I'm very sorry."

"What do you mean?" Brennan's voice pitched higher. "Where is she?"

The policeman's face dropped. He glanced at his

partner before answering. "I hate to tell you this, but she didn't survive the crash." He paused, letting the words settle. "An ambulance is coming now. But there won't be anything they can do except recover her body."

"Recover her body?" The words came out as a whisper first. Then Brennan repeated them, louder. "Recover her body?"

His knees buckled.

Rita and Callie reached him at the same time, each taking an arm, holding him upright. His weight sagged between them. Through his shirt sleeve, Callie felt him trembling.

The ambulance rounded the final curve, its siren cutting off mid-wail as it rolled to a stop. Two paramedics jumped out, moving with practiced efficiency even though everyone present knew there was no rush. Not anymore.

A silver Mazda CX3 came along the road from up the hill. It pulled onto the narrow shoulder, tires crunching gravel, and the driver stepped out.

Tommy Valdez.

Valdez ran up to Callie. "Haylie?" He looked from her to the police cars to the officers at the precipice. "What are you doing here? What's going on?"

Callie gently released Brennan's arm, letting Rita support him alone. She stepped away, drawing Valdez with her, and filled him in with what little she knew. Her voice stayed low, but each word landed with weight.

"An accident?" Valdez's hand went to his chest. "Oh no! I knew this curve was too dangerous. People drive it much too fast." He rubbed his hand through his hair, looking around as if seeing the road as a thing of evil. "I've lived in fear that this would happen, and now it has."

He turned back toward the scene. His eyes widened.

"Wait!" He grabbed Callie's arm. "Is that Marcus Brennan?" His voice dropped to a whisper. "This couldn't be his wife, could it?"

"I'm sad to say, it was."

"Oh, no." Valdez wrung his hands, twisting his fingers together. "How much tragedy can one man endure? First his horse and now this!" He looked at Callie, then back at Brennan. "I need to go talk to him."

Callie watched Valdez walk up to Brennan and tap him on the shoulder. When the younger man turned, his face streaked with tears, Valdez pulled him into an embrace. He held Brennan in a tight hug, neither man speaking. Brennan buried his head in Valdez's shoulder, and his body shook with sobs. Valdez's hand moved in slow circles on Brennan's back.

They stood like that for several minutes while the paramedics began their descent down the embankment.

Chapter 52

Less than twenty-four hours later, Callie received another call from Rita Kowalski.

"Callie." The detective's voice was tense. "I have some disturbing news for you."

Callie caught her breath. She set down the glass of water she was holding. "What is it?"

"Dianne Brennan's death wasn't an accident."

The words hung in the air.

"What?" Callie's hand tightened on the phone. "How can that be?"

"Her brake line had been cut."

Callie blanched.

Paul and Callie were having lunch at the Ashville

Diner when the call from Rita came in. Paul saw Callie's face go white—all the color draining from her cheeks in an instant. He set down his fork, mouthed across the table, "What is it?"

Callie punched off her phone and kept staring, wide-eyed, not responding. Her mind a jumble of confusing thoughts that wouldn't line up properly. Cut brake line. Murder. Marcus Brennan's face. Tommy Valdez appearing on that curve.

"Callie." Paul leaned forward. "What is it?"

Callie shook her head in disbelief. She set down the sandwich she was holding, unable to remember picking it up. "Paul, that was Rita Kowalski." She swallowed. "She said Dianne Brennan's accident wasn't an accident at all. Someone cut her brake line." She looked up at him. "She was murdered."

It took Paul several minutes to digest the news. Then his reporter instincts took control. He sat back against the vinyl booth, his mind already working through the possibilities, sorting facts from speculation.

"We need to find out who did that." He pulled out his notebook, flipping to a clean page. "One thing we know is that it couldn't have been Frank Morrison. He's still in custody."

Thinking about the dangerous curves on Valley View Drive, Paul added. "It couldn't have happened before she drove up that road. She would never have made it around those curves."

"And it couldn't have been her husband." Callie's voice was barely above a whisper. "He was with us."

Paul nodded, deep in thought. "Then the question is, where had she been right before the accident?"

With the cooperation of Rita Kowalski, who reluctantly agreed to help them, Callie and Paul were able to get the phone company to release Dianne

Brennan's cell phone records for the past several months. They spread the printouts across Paul's dining room table, the pages covering nearly every inch of space. "That woman loved to use her cell phone," Paul said.

They were able to identify Marcus Brennan's number easily—it appeared hundreds of times. Then the numbers of friends, her mother and sister, a hair salon, the gym, the therapist she mentioned in her Facebook post. Most were typical calls a young woman would make.

Shortly after the fire at the track, they noticed one number appearing frequently. Not surprisingly, with all they had learned about the blackmail scheme going on, that number belonged to Frank Morrison. The calls were brief, only a minute or two with the exception of the very first call. It lasted over ten minutes.

But there was another number that kept popping up, beginning first before the July 6th fire and with unusual frequency the last few days.

Paul circled it with red ink. "This one."

Callie leaned over his shoulder, studying the pattern. The calls were longer, some lasting twenty minutes or more. And they usually came in the middle of the afternoon.

But the very last call she had made was to that number the very morning of her death.

"We need to find out who this is," Callie said.

Paul was already reaching for his phone.

Twenty minutes later, they had a name and an address.

They decided to pay a visit to the owner of that number.

At the crest of the hill, two stately brick columns marked the entrance to the home. The brass numbers on the columns matched the address Paul had scribbled into his notebook. "This is it." Paul turned onto the curved driveway, the old truck looking out of place in such an elegant setting.

The approach stretched before them—pristine asphalt bordered by dormant flowerbeds, winter-bare maples standing sentinel on either side. Paul pulled up to the circular turnaround and cut the engine. The red brick Georgian sat solid and imposing, its symmetrical façade watching them with dark-eyed windows.

He turned to Callie. "You've been awfully quiet.

Having second thoughts?"

"Second, third, and fourth."

Callie looked out the passenger window at the imposing house with its double front doors, their glossy black paint reflecting weak afternoon sun. One of those cute antique cast iron jockeys with colorfully painted silks stood by the entrance, one white-gloved hand extended, holding a painted ring. *Tie your horse and come in,* it seemed to say.

Callie took a deep breath and gathered her strength. "Let's do this. We need to find out if he is involved once and for all."

The brick walkway led them past dormant rosebushes wrapped in burlap. Paul pressed the doorbell. A melodic chime echoed somewhere deep inside the house.

Footsteps, heels on marble, approached. The door opened.

An attractive middle-aged woman, dark hair and eyes, dressed in a comfortable cream cable-knit sweater and charcoal slacks stood in the threshold. One hand gripped the door's brass handle. Her posture radiated the comfortable authority of someone at home in spaces like this.

Her head cocked to one side as she looked Callie over. Then her expression softened and the corner of her mouth quirked up.

"Miss Norr." She smiled. "How good to see you. Won't you come in?"

She stepped aside, gesturing them into a two-story foyer where afternoon light filtered through a fanlight transom, scattering diamonds across white marble veined with gray.

"Thank you, Mrs. Valdez." Callie crossed the threshold, Paul close behind. "This is my friend, Paul Coffman."

"Of course." Mrs. Valdez extended her hand to Paul.

"The reporter. My husband always appreciates your columns—especially when they're about one of our horses." She smiled and her eyes twinkled.

Paul returned the smile and nodded, accepting her handshake. "Pleasure to meet you."

"We were hoping to visit with Tommy," Callie said.

Mrs. Valdez's face fell. "Oh dear. I'm afraid you've missed him."

"Is he at the track?" Callie asked.

"No, dear." She shook her head, a small apologetic gesture. "He is on his way to the Philadelphia airport. Left about an hour ago. He's flying to Canada—Ontario. Wants to check out a horse he's interested in."

Callie reached into her jacket pocket, withdrew a photograph. She held it out. "Do you recognize this woman?"

Mrs. Valdez took the photo. Her mouth turned down, eyelids drooping as sorrow settled over her face. "Of course. That is Marcus Brennan's wife." She looked up, eyes glistening. "Oh dear, what a tragedy. And she was here—right in this house—just before her accident." Her voice dropped. "I even served her tea. We had such a nice visit while we waited for Tommy to return."

Paul's posture changed, sharpened. "Return?"

"Yes." Mrs. Valdez's gaze drifted toward a pair of closed double doors to the right of the foyer. Dark wood, brass hardware catching the light. "They were having a meeting in his office. Tommy asked me to entertain her while he handled some important business. He went out to his car and left us to visit until he returned."

"Was he gone long?" Callie kept her voice even, casual.

"Oh no. Not long at all. Only about ten minutes." Mrs. Valdez handed the photograph back. "I so enjoyed visiting with her. We talked about our husbands' love of horses. I expressed my sorrow at the loss of Dusty and

Thunder in the fire and asked how her husband was taking the loss." She pressed her lips together. "I can't tell you how shocked I was to learn of her death. Such a sad, sad day."

Callie suddenly felt too warm. The sadness weighing on her as well. She slipped the photo back into her pocket.

"I should mention that I was concerned about her when she left."

Callie looked up. "Concerned?"

"Yes. She complained of being so tired. I offered to call an Uber for her, but she insisted that she would be fine—just needed to get home and take a rest." Mrs. Valdez dropped her chin and shook her head. "I can't help thinking this was my fault for not insisting that she get a driver."

Callie reached out and clasped her hand. "You shouldn't blame yourself. You couldn't have known."

"When will Tommy return?" Paul asked.

Turning to him, Mrs. Valdez lifted one shoulder in an elegant shrug. "I really can't say. He said he'd let me know. You know how these buying trips go. One farm leads to another, one bloodline to the next. When he goes on these horse-buying trips, one never knows where he will end up."

Callie squeezed Mrs. Valdez's hand in both of hers. The older woman's fingers were warm and soft. "Thank you for your time, Mrs. Valdez. We'll be going now."

"Oh, do come back and visit properly." Mrs. Valdez hung onto Callie's hand a bit longer. "And tell me how Sunny is doing. I'm so glad you have recovered from that awful accident." Her free hand rose to her chest. "I watched the whole thing from our box. It scared the living daylights out of me."

"Thank you for your concern. I'm fine now." She glanced at Paul, saw the tension in his jaw. "We best be going."

"Yes." Paul nodded to Mrs. Valdez. "Nice to meet you, Mrs. Valdez. Thank you for your time."

Mrs. Valdez walked them to the door, stood framed in the threshold as they descended the brick steps. The cast-iron jockey watched them leave, hand extended in frozen farewell.

Neither spoke until they reached the truck.

Paul opened Callie's door, waited for her to settle in before closing it and circled to the driver's side. The engine turned over. He shifted into reverse but didn't move yet.

"Ten minutes," he said.

"Long enough to cut brake lines," Callie said.

She looked back at the house, Mrs. Valdez's silhouette withdrawing from the doorway as the double doors closed. "He's leaving the country."

"Yes."

"I'm calling Rita. Maybe they can stop him at the airport."

The newsroom at the Ashville Gazette was empty that night except for one lone reporter hunched over his computer keyboard. The lamplight sent a halo around his face, showing his frown as he concentrated on perhaps his biggest story yet.

Chapter 54

Tommy Valdez sat alone in the interrogation room tucked into the back corner of Ashville's cramped police headquarters. The space reeked of institutional neglect—scuffed linoleum, a scratched metal table bolted to the floor, walls that might once have been white, now stained to a cheerless beige. Overhead, fluorescent tubes buzzed and flickered, casting unstable shadows across his face.

Through the one-way glass, Callie stood between Paul and Rita, watching Valdez's fingers drum an anxious rhythm against the tabletop. A bead of sweat traced the line of his temple, hesitated at his jaw, then dropped onto his collar.

Rita pulled out a pen and notepad. She clicked the pen once. Twice. "Time to read him his rights, then we'll see what he has to say."

The detective stepped around the corner, her unhurried gait showing her confidence. Paul and Callie watched through the glass as she entered the room.

Rita pulled out the chair directly across from Valdez. Metal scraped against tile. She sat. Valdez looked up.

"Mr. Valdez. I'm Detective Rita Kowalski. We met briefly during the initial investigation of the fire at Liberty Racetrack."

"I remember." His knee bounced beneath the table. "Why did the cops pull me out of the airport just as I was about to board my plane? I was already cleared through security, boarding pass in hand…" His attempt at control did nothing to hide his rancor.

Rita set her notebook on the table and folded her hands on top of it. "Before we discuss that, I need to read you your rights." She pulled a card from her jacket pocket and began reading in a measured tone.

"You have the right to remain silent. Anything you say can and will be used against you in a court of law. You have the right to an attorney. If you cannot afford an attorney, one will be provided for you. Do you understand these rights as I have read them to you?"

Valdez's knee stopped bouncing. "What is this about? What am I being charged with?"

"Do you understand your rights, Mr. Valdez?"

"Yes, yes. I understand." He waved his hand dismissively. "Now tell me what this is about."

Rita leaned back in her chair, her expression neutral. "We have reason to believe you are connected to the fire at Liberty Racetrack on July 6th of this year, and to the death of Dianne Brennan."

"Death?" Valdez's hands gripped the edge of the table. "She died in a car accident. Everyone knows that."

"Did she?" Rita opened her notebook, flipping to a marked page. "Let's start with something simpler. Can you explain your relationship with Mrs. Brennan?"

"She was married to Marcus. I knew them both from the track." His answer came too quickly.

Rita pulled out a stack of papers, spreading them across the table in a neat fan. "These are phone records, Mr. Valdez. Your phone records and Mrs. Brennan's. Beginning two weeks before the fire, the two of you exchanged numerous calls." She tapped one highlighted section. "Some lasting twenty minutes or more. That's quite a bit of time for casual acquaintances."

Valdez's jaw tightened. "Her marriage was falling apart. Marcus was obsessed with that horse. She needed someone to talk to, someone who understood the harness racing world."

"I see." Rita made a note. "And you were that someone."

"I was trying to help."

"Help." Rita let the word hang in the air. "Interesting choice of words." She flipped to another page. "After the fire, the calls stopped for a long period of time. Why was that?"

Valdez shifted in his seat. "The horse was dead. Marcus started paying attention to her again. The marriage problems solved themselves."

"Solved themselves," Rita repeated, writing something down. "But then, just a few days ago, the calls started up again." She looked up, meeting his eyes. "Three calls in the two days before her death. The last one the morning she died. What were those calls about, Mr. Valdez?"

"I don't remember. Probably just checking in, seeing how she was doing."

"Twenty-three minutes seems like a long check-in call."

Valdez's hands moved from the table to his lap. "Look, I don't know what you're trying to imply, but-"

"I'm not implying anything yet. I'm simply trying to understand the nature of your relationship with Mrs. Brennan." Rita pulled out another document. "Let's talk about Eat My Dust."

The change in subject made Valdez blink. "What about him?"

"You took out a five-hundred-thousand-dollar insurance policy on him sixteen days before the fire."

"So? He was valuable. Of course I insured him."

"Interesting timing, though." Rita consulted her notes. "According to Dr. Paige Taylor's veterinary records, she examined Eat My Dust three days before the fire. Her diagnosis was a completely torn suspensory ligament and bone chips in one front leg. Career-ending injuries."

Valdez's face flushed. "That's not—she must have made a mistake."

"Dr. Taylor is a licensed veterinarian with fifteen years of experience. She documented everything thoroughly." Rita paused. "Except her file on Eat My Dust went missing from your barn office. Do you know anything about that?"

"No."

"No?" Rita pulled out yet another document. "We also have records showing you contacted several of Ashville's wealthiest businesspeople shortly before the fire. Would you like to tell me what those calls were about?"

Valdez said nothing, his lips pressed into a thin line.

"I'll tell you what they told us. You were selling shares in Eat My Dust. Premium shares in a horse you knew would never race again." Rita leaned forward slightly. "That's fraud, Mr. Valdez."

"I gave them their money back after the fire!"

"Because you had to. Because a dead horse can't race, and an injured horse you were hiding couldn't be syndicated." Rita's voice remained calm, almost conversational. "But here's what I find interesting. You owed money to Joey Castellano. Significant money. The syndication was going to solve that problem, but then the horse broke down. The insurance policy was your backup plan."

"You can't prove any of this."

"Can't I?" Rita pulled out a photograph, sliding it across the table. "Do you recognize this?"

Valdez glanced at it. The photo showed Frank Morrison standing next to JT Walters at the track's Christmas party. "So. It's a party photo."

"A photo that you took."

"Yeah. So what?"

"Look at it more carefully." Rita tapped the image. "This is the original. We found it on your computer photos."

"I made copies for everyone and passed them out."

"We found a cropped version of this photo—just showing JT—tucked into a threatening letter left on Haylie Norr's windshield. The letter tried to frame JT for cutting the line on her sulky before the Maple Leaf Pace."

"I don't know anything about that. Many people have that photo."

"But it was only your fingerprints that we found on the envelope, Mr. Valdez."

The color drained from his face.

Behind the glass, Callie felt Paul's hand find hers and squeeze.

Rita gathered her papers slowly, deliberately. "Here's what I think happened. You convinced Dianne Brennan to start the fire. You manipulated a desperate, grieving woman who was losing her husband to his obsession with a horse. You promised her it would solve her problems. And when Frank Morrison started blackmailing her over it, she came to you for help."

"That's insane. You're making up stories—"

"Am I? Rita stood. "We have phone records connecting you to Dianne Brennan before and after the fire. We have evidence you were committing insurance fraud. We have your fingerprints on a letter designed to frame an innocent man. And we have forensic evidence from the morning Dianne Brennan died." She leaned forward, palms flat on the table. "Her brake lines were cut, Mr. Valdez. This wasn't an accident. It was murder."

Valdez shot to his feet.

"I want a lawyer. Right now. I'm not saying another word."

Chapter 55

Rita straightened, her expression unchanged. "That's your right." She walked to the door, then paused. "You'll be held here until your attorney arrives. I suggest you use that time to think very carefully about your situation."

She stepped out, closing the door with a decisive click.

In the viewing room, Callie let out a long breath as Rita entered.

"What happens now?" Paul asked.

"Now we wait." Rita tucked her notebook under her

arm. "He's asked for counsel, so all questioning stops until his attorney arrives. But I laid out enough that his lawyer will know exactly what kind of evidence we have. Smart attorneys start thinking about deals when they see a case this strong."

"You think he'll make a deal?" Callie asked.

Rita glanced back at the glass where Tommy Valdez sat slumped in his chair, head in his hands. "I think once his attorney sees everything we have, a deal might be the only play they've got."

Two hours later, a man in an expensive gray suit and perfectly knotted blue tie strode through the police station's front doors. His leather briefcase looked like it cost more than most people's monthly rent, and the diamond ring on his left hand caught the fluorescent lights as he approached the desk sergeant.

"Edward Daines, attorney at law. I'm here for Thomas Valdez."

Behind the glass, Callie, Paul, and Rita watched as Daines was shown to the interrogation room. The lawyer's face was impassive as he entered, but his eyes moved quickly, cataloging everything.

"Mr. Valdez." Daines set his briefcase on the table. "I'm Edward Daines. Your wife retained me on your behalf."

Valdez looked up, relief flooding his face. "Thank you for coming. You have to get me out of here. They're accusing me of murder. Murder! It's completely ridiculous. I haven't done anything wrong. They have no evidence—"

Daines held up one hand, silencing him. "Mr. Valdez, the first rule when dealing with law enforcement is this: stop talking." He pulled out a legal pad and pen. "I'll do the talking from now on. You only talk to me. Understood?"

Valdez nodded mutely.

"Good." Daines settled into the chair, crossing one leg over the other. "Now, I need you to tell me everything, and I mean everything, from the beginning. Don't leave anything out, and for heaven's sake, don't lie to me. I can't help you if I don't know what I'm dealing with."

For the next hour, Callie and Paul watched through the glass as Valdez talked and Daines took notes. They couldn't hear the conversation, but they could see Daines' expression growing progressively darker. At one point, the attorney set down his pen and rubbed his temples. At another, he stood and paced the small room.

When Valdez finally stopped talking, Daines returned to his seat and stared at his client for a long moment.

"Mr. Valdez," he said quietly, "You are in serious trouble."

Chapter 56

Rita's phone buzzed. "Kowalski." Rita listened, her face stoic. She nodded her head, listened some more, then, "Thank you. That's all I need to finish this. Send it up."

Five minutes later, as Valdez and his attorney continued to consult in a back room, a uniformed officer appeared with a thick manila folder. Rita flipped through it, her expression unreadable, then pulled out several documents.

"This just came from the lab." She showed Paul and Callie the top sheet. "Autopsy report on Dianne Brennan.

They found Dormisol in her bloodstream—a prescription sedative that causes drowsiness and impairs reaction time."

"Could she have taken it herself?" Paul asked.

"She had no prescription for it." Rita flipped to another page. "However, Mrs. Valdez does. And look at this." She pulled out a second report. "Forensics tested the teacup Mrs. Valdez used to serve Mrs. Brennan. It hadn't been washed yet. They found traces of Dormisol in it."

Callie's stomach dropped. "Did Mrs. Valdez drug her?"

"Possibly, if she knew what was going on. But my gut tells me no. I believe Tommy Valdez drugged her." Pulling out another sheet of paper Rita added, "And this is from the crime scene techs who processed the driveway. They found brake fluid—the same viscosity, same brand, as what was in Dianne Brennan's car. The stain pattern is consistent with it dripping from cut lines."

"That's premeditated murder," Paul said.

"Yes, it is." Rita closed the folder. "Time to let Mr. Daines know exactly what his client is facing."

Rita knocked once on the interrogation room door, then entered. Daines looked up, his expression wary.

"Mr. Daines. I'm Detective Kowalski. I thought you should see the evidence we've compiled." Rita set the folder on the table. "These reports came in from the lab just a few minutes ago."

Daines pulled the folder toward him and began reading. His face, which had already been grim, turned ashen as he worked through the documents.

"These are autopsy results," he said quietly.

"Yes. Showing Dormisol in Mrs. Brennan's system. Dormisol was also found in a teacup from your client's home." Rita remained standing. "We also have forensic evidence from his driveway—brake fluid from Mrs. Brennan's car."

Daines looked at Valdez, who had gone very still in his chair.

"This is a death penalty case, Mr. Daines. Premeditated murder with aggravating circumstances—arson resulting in multiple deaths and massive property damage." Rita's voice was matter-of-fact. "The DA is already preparing the paperwork."

Daines closed the folder carefully. "Detective, I need time to consult with my client. Alone."

"Of course." Rita left the room.

Behind the glass, Callie watched as Daines turned to Valdez. Even without audio, she could read the attorney's body language—the set of the shoulders, the way he leaned forward, the sharp gestures as he explained the situation.

Valdez's head dropped into his hands.

Twenty minutes later, Daines emerged and found Rita in the hallway. "Detective, I'd like to speak with the prosecutor handling this case."

Chapter 57

The conference room was barely larger than the interrogation room, but at least it had a window. Late afternoon sun slanted through dusty venetian blinds, casting stripes across the scarred table where Edward Daines sat across from District Attorney Neil Lathen.

Valdez was just starting his fourth day in custody at the county jail when the powers that be met to discuss his fate.

Rita Kowalski sat at the end of the table, her case file open before her. Callie and Paul waited in the hallway outside, close enough to be called in if needed.

"Let's not waste each other's time," Lathen said, settling into his chair. He was younger than Callie had expected when she'd glimpsed him earlier—maybe forty, with sharp eyes and wire-rimmed glasses. "Your client is looking at first-degree murder, multiple counts of conspiracy to commit arson resulting in death, insurance fraud, and obstruction of justice. I'm going for the death penalty."

Daines didn't flinch. "My client is willing to cooperate fully."

"Cooperate how?" Lathen asked.

"Full confession. Complete details of how the fire was planned and executed, his role in Dianne Brennan's death, everything." Daines pulled out his own legal pad. "In exchange, you take the death penalty off the table."

Lathen leaned back, studying the defense attorney. "That's a big ask for someone facing what your client is facing."

"You'll get a clean conviction. No trial, no risk of jury nullification or appeal based on trial errors. My client pleads guilty, a complete confession, and you put this to bed." Daines tapped his pen on the pad.

"Life without parole. That's my offer." Lathen sat back.

"Life with the possibility of parole after twenty-five years."

"Thirty-five, and that's as low as I go." Lathen crossed his arms. "Twenty-eight horses died in that fire, Mr. Daines. Twenty-eight. Not to mention the destruction of property and the murder of Dianne Brennan. Your client really doesn't deserve to see the light of day again."

Daines was quiet for a moment. "I'll discuss this with my client."

"You've got one hour." Lathen stood. "After that, the offer expires and we proceed to trial. And I *will* get the death penalty, Mr. Daines. This case is airtight."

Chapter 58

Rita found Callie and Paul in the hallway. "Lathen's offering life with possibility of parole after thirty-five years. Daines is taking it to Valdez now."

"Will he take it?" Callie asked.

"If he's smart." Rita checked her watch. "The alternative is a needle in his arm. Even with automatic appeals, Pennsylvania's death row is not somewhere you want to end up."

They waited. The hallway clock ticked. Somewhere in the building, a phone rang. Footsteps echoed in the stairwell.

Forty-five minutes later, Daines emerged from the interrogation room. His face was drawn, exhausted.

"My client accepts the terms."

The formal confession session began at 6:00 p.m. The interrogation room felt different now—less adversarial, more procedural. A video camera had been set up in the corner, its red light glowing. A court stenographer sat to one side, fingers poised over her machine.

Rita sat across from Valdez, with District Attorney Lathen beside her. Daines sat next to his client, a thick stack of papers before him—the plea agreement, signed and notarized.

Rita started the recording. "This is Detective Rita Kowalski. Present are District Attorney Neil Lathen, defense attorney Edward Daines, court reporter Karen Schick, and the defendant, Thomas Valdez. Mr. Valdez, you've been advised of your rights, correct?"

"Yes."

"And you're waiving those rights voluntarily to provide this statement?"

Valdez glanced at Daines, who nodded. "Yes."

"For the record, please state your full name and date of birth."

"Thomas Miguel Valdez. July 14, 1978."

Rita opened her notebook. "Mr. Valdez, you've agreed to provide a full and complete account of events related to the fire at Liberty Racetrack on July 6, 2026, and the death of Dianne Brennan. Is that correct?"

"Yes."

"Let's begin with your relationship with Mrs. Brennan. When did you first meet her?"

Valdez took a breath. His hands lay flat on the table, fingers spread. "About two years ago. Through the track. She was Marcus Brennan's wife."

"When did your relationship become more than casual acquaintance?"

"Last June. Early June." He paused. "She called me one day, very upset. Said she needed to talk to someone who would understand."

"Understand what?"

"What it's like with someone obsessed with horses." Valdez's voice was flat, emotionless. "Marcus had purchased Thunder's Echo the year before. The horse was doing well—winning races, building value. But Marcus had quit his job and was spending every free moment at the barn. He'd get home late at night, leave again at five in the morning. She felt invisible."

"What did you tell her?"

"At first, just what she wanted to hear. That it would pass, that the racing season would end, that Marcus would come around." Valdez shifted in his chair. "But the more we talked, the more I realized she was desperate. She'd lost a baby a couple of months earlier. Marcus didn't know how to deal with her grief, so he threw himself into the horse even harder."

Rita made a note. "When did the conversation turn to the fire?"

Valdez was silent for several seconds. "The beginning of July. I'd just found out about Dusty's injury. Dr. Taylor had done the exam, found the torn ligament and bone chips. The horse was finished."

"But you didn't tell anyone about the injury."

"No." His jaw tightened. "I took the file from the barn office. Hid it at my house. I'd already taken out the insurance policy—"

"The five-hundred-thousand-dollar policy," Rita interjected.

"Yes. I'd taken it out two weeks earlier, thinking it would protect my investment if anything happened. But when Dusty broke down, I realized..." He trailed off.

"Realized what, Mr. Valdez?"

"That I couldn't syndicate a lame horse. And Numbers...I mean Joey Castellano...was breathing down my neck for fifty thousand dollars. I had two weeks to pay him or..." Another pause. "He made it clear what would happen if I didn't pay."

"So, you decided to collect on the insurance policy."

"I started thinking about it." Valdez rubbed his face with both hands. "The policy would pay out if the horse died. But I couldn't just shoot him—that would be obvious fraud. It had to look like an accident."

"A fire," Rita said.

"A fire." Valdez's voice dropped to barely above a whisper. "Barn fires happen. Everyone in racing knows that. Bad wiring, hay combustion, someone's careless cigarette. They happen."

"But this fire wouldn't just happen. You needed someone to start it."

"Yes."

"And you chose Dianne Brennan."

Valdez nodded slowly. "She called me one night, crying. Said she couldn't take it anymore. Said she'd kicked him out of the house. Said she'd do anything to get him back, to make him see what he was losing." He looked up, meeting Rita's eyes. "I told her I knew a way."

Behind the glass, Callie felt sick. Paul gave her a quick hug before returning to his note taking.

"What exactly did you tell her?" Rita asked.

"I said if the horse were gone, Marcus would have nothing left to obsess over. He'd return to her." Valdez's voice had gone hollow. "I made it sound like I was helping her save her marriage. Like it was a blessing for everyone involved."

"But you were really setting up a scenario where your horse would die, too, triggering the insurance payout."

"Yes."

"How did you convince her to actually do it?"

"I gave her the supplies. Told her exactly what to do." Valdez described the milk jug, the gasoline, the sock as the wick, the white grocery bag to carry it all in. "I even pulled the hay bale in front of Thunder's stall. I told her to wait until after JT's midnight rounds, when he'd be back in the office. Told her to enter from the back, place the jug just in front of the hay bale, light the wick, and leave. The sock would burn for ten to fifteen minutes before reaching the gasoline, giving her time to get away."

"Did you tell her about the other horses in the barn?"

A long pause. "Not really."

"You didn't mention that twenty-seven other horses would die?"

"I told her that the fire would be noticed quickly and would be put out before it spread to the other horses."

"But you knew that wasn't true," Rita said.

Valdez looked down at his hands. "Yes."

"You told her what she needed to hear to get her to do it."

"Yes."

"But you knew it would spread."

Valdez said nothing.

"You knew your horse would die."

"Yes." His voice cracked slightly. "But I also knew the insurance would pay out. I'd be clear of my debt to Castellano. I could start over."

"Except the insurance company didn't pay immediately."

"No. They wanted to investigate after the fire marshal determined the fire was started by arson." Valdez's hands clenched into fists. "I had to find another way to pay Castellano. That's when I entered Magic in the Maple Leaf Pace. I bet everything I had left on her, and she won. I paid off my debt."

"So, you didn't need the insurance money anymore," Rita said.

"No. But by then, things had gotten complicated."

"Complicated how?"

"Frank Morrison." Valdez spat the name. "He'd kept the surveillance footage from that night. He saw Dianne on the tape, carrying the bag toward the barns. He confronted her, told her he'd go to the police unless she paid him."

"How did you find out about this?"

"Dianne called me, panicking. Said Morrison wanted twenty-five thousand dollars." Valdez rubbed his eyes. "I told her to pay it. Told her it would buy his silence."

"But it didn't."

"No. After Morrison came back for more money, she called me and wanted to meet. Said she'd tell the police everything if I didn't help her pay. She'd tell them it was my idea, that I'd manipulated her into doing it." His voice hardened. "She said if she was going down, she was taking me with her."

Rita leaned forward. "That's when you decided to kill her."

"I didn't want to." The words came quickly. "I just wanted her to stay quiet. But she wouldn't listen. She was falling apart."

"So, you invited her to your house."

"Yes. Wednesday morning. Told her I'd have money for her and that we'd figure out what to do with Morrison." Valdez's voice had gone flat again, reciting facts without emotion. "When she arrived, I took her into my office. Offered her ten thousand. She said she wanted twenty-five thousand to match what she had already paid Morrison. Said it was my fault she was in this mess. That I owed her."

"What did you say?"

"I told her I'd get the money. Asked her to wait while I made some calls." He paused. "I went upstairs to my bedroom. My wife keeps sleeping pills in the medicine cabinet—Dormisol. I crushed two tablets into powder."

"And then?"

"I went back downstairs, called my wife in from the kitchen. Asked her to make tea and keep Dianne company while I went out to my car to get my phone." His breathing had grown shallow. "When my wife wasn't looking, I stirred the powder into Dianne's tea."

"Then you went outside."

"Yes. Dianne's car was in the driveway. It took me less than five minutes." He described crawling under the vehicle, locating the brake lines, using wire cutters to slice through the metal braiding. "I cut them half way through. Enough that they'd hold for a few miles of normal driving, but as soon as she needed to brake hard…"

"You cut the steering linkage too."

"Yes. I wanted to make sure that even if she realized the brakes weren't working, she couldn't steer out of trouble." No emotion in his voice. Just mechanics. "Valley View Drive has those sharp curves. I knew if the brakes failed on one of those turns, she wouldn't make it."

"Then you came back inside."

"Yes. The pills were already taking effect. Dianne kept saying how tired she felt. My wife offered to call her an Uber, but Dianne insisted she just needed to get home and rest." Valdez's hands trembled slightly. "I watched her drive away, knowing what would happen."

The room fell silent except for the soft clicking of the stenographer's machine.

Rita pulled out the photograph of Dianne Brennan— a picture taken at the memorial service, where she was smiling, leaning against her husband. "This woman trusted you. She came to you for help."

"I know."

"And you killed her."

"If Morrison hadn't…"

Daines reached over and placed his hand on Valdez's

arm, stopping him.

Rita closed her notebook. "One more question. The letter left on Callie Oaks' windshield—the one designed to frame JT Walters. Tell me about that."

Valdez's shoulders sagged. "I found out she was investigating for the insurance company. Working undercover as Haylie Norr. I thought I could scare her off, make her think she was in danger so she'd stop digging. I didn't want to hurt her—I swear. I cut the line carefully so it would break during the race but wouldn't cause a serious accident."

"But it did cause a serious accident. She and the horse could have been killed."

"I know." For the first time something like remorse flickered across his face. "I'm sorry. For all of it. For the horses, for Dianne, for Callie." He looked directly at the camera. "I'm so sorry."

Chapter 59

ASHVILLE GAZETTE-SPORTS

**LOCAL BREEDER ADMITS TO
MURDER AND ARSON**
By Paul Coffman

ASHVILLE, PA – Local breeder Tommy Valdez admitted to being involved in the plot to start the fire at Liberty Racetrack on July 6th of this year and to causing the death of local woman, Dianne Brennan, to cover it up...

The next morning arrived with a layer of snow that had fallen during the night, covering the world with a blanket of white. Callie drove toward Liberty Racetrack and thought how fitting it was. White, purity, cleanliness. Something her world desperately needed right now.

She had barely slept. Every time she closed her eyes, she saw Tommy Valdez's face in that interrogation room—the emptiness in his eyes as he described how he'd murdered Dianne Brennan. The horses.

Paul had left the police station as soon as it was over to write his story. No doubt he'd spent the night at the office. Some truths, Callie thought, were too heavy for words.

Now, standing in Barn 6 with Sunny nuzzling her shoulder, Callie tried to find her way back to normal…whatever normal meant anymore.

"Thought I'd find you here." Stanley Smithfield came up behind her.

Callie turned. The trainer looked as tired as she felt. "Couldn't sleep."

"Same." Stanley moved to Sunny's stall and reached up to scratch behind the filly's ears. "Been up since two, just sitting in my kitchen, trying to make sense of it all."

"Any luck?"

"Not a bit." He pulled a carrot from his jacket pocket and offered it to Sunny on a flat palm. The filly took it delicately, her soft lips barely touching his skin. "Twenty-eight horses, Haylie. Or should I say, Callie."

Callie could only nod.

"I keep thinking about them," he continued. "About Thunder, Dusty, and all the others. About the fact that they died because one man couldn't face his own mistakes."

"And because a woman couldn't face losing her husband." Callie stroked Sunny's neck.

"Evil." Stanley's voice was flat. "That's the only word for it. Pure evil."

"The sentencing has been set for December 15th. At least it won't be a long trial."

A door slammed outside. Footsteps approached. Paul appeared in the barn entrance, two cups of hot cocoa in his hands. "Thought you might need this."

Callie took the offered cup gratefully. The warmth seeped into her palms. "You're a life saver."

"I try." Paul nodded to Stanley. "Morning."

"Morning Paul. You look like you had a long night, too."

"No sleep for me."

"Well, I should get to work. Got three horses to jog this morning and Magic needs her hooves trimmed." He paused at the stall door. "Callie, you still planning to keep working as my assistant?"

The question caught her off guard. With the investigation over, Schmidt was expecting her to return to Mutual Assurance as a claims investigator. It hadn't occurred to her to stay at the track. "I…I don't know. Do you think I should?"

"I think those horses who died deserve to be remembered. And the best way to honor them is to keep doing what you do best—keep training, keep racing, keep loving these amazing animals."

 **Epilogue**

Six months later, the spring sun warmed Callie's shoulders as she guided Sunny through the final turn at Liberty Racetrack. The filly's stride was powerful and confident, her lateral gait eating up ground with that distinctive wobble that marked a seasoned pacer. No hesitation. No fear. Just pure, focused determination.

They crossed the finish line and Callie eased back on the lines, letting Sunny slow to a jog, then a walk. Her heart swelled with pride. The filly had come so far from that terrified horse who'd bolted over the rail last fall.

When she called Carson Schmidt to tell him she wasn't returning to Mutual Assurance, he had done his best to convince her to stay. The way she felt right now told her definitively that she had made the right decision.

Stanley Smithfield was waiting at the gap, stopwatch in hand, a grin splitting his weathered face. "1:52 flat. That's her best time yet."

Callie brought Sunny to a halt and climbed down from the sulky, her legs slightly unsteady after the adrenaline rush. She ran her hand down Sunny's neck, feeling the mare's muscles quiver beneath her sweat-dampened coat. "She's ready."

"More than ready." Stanley clipped a lead rope to Sunny's bridle. "The Meadow Vale Stakes is in two weeks. I think we should enter her."

"Really?" Callie's voice rose with excitement despite herself. A stakes race.

It didn't seem that long ago that she'd wondered if Sunny would ever race again.

"Really." Stanley's expression grew serious. "You've done remarkable work with her, Callie. I mean that."

She noticed he'd used her real name—something that had taken weeks to adjust to after the investigation concluded. Most people at the track knew the truth now. Haylie Norr had been quietly retired, and Callie Oaks had taken her place. To her relief, the backstretch community had been more forgiving than she'd expected. They understood why she'd done what she'd done.

"I couldn't have done it without you," Callie said. "You taught me everything."

"You came with the mechanics." Stanley started walking Sunny toward the barn, Callie falling into step beside him. "I just fine-tuned it a bit. But you had the heart for it all along." He paused, his jaw working. "I still can't believe Tommy..." His voice trailed off.

They'd had this conversation several times before, but Callie knew Stanley needed to process it again. And again. The betrayal still cut deep.

"I started working with him just over a year ago," Stanley said, rubbing his forehead with his palm. "But I'd been watching him for years before that. I took the job as his driver because I thought I knew him."

"We all did. He was good at hiding who he really was." She placed her hand on his arm. "Stanley, there is something I have been meaning to ask you about."

"What's that?"

"Now that Tommy is in jail, what will happen to the horses? We have been carrying on as if nothing had changed. But everything has changed. What will happen to them?" She reached over and rested her hand on Sunny's shoulder. "To Sunny?"

"I've been talking with Mrs. Valdez. We're working out a partnership where we'll have joint ownership of the harness racing business." He stopped Sunny and turned toward Callie. "She's willing to cut you in if you want. You could be part owner of Sunny."

Callie's mouth dropped open. "Really?" She threw her arms around Stanley. Then pulled back in embarrassment. Her hand flew to her mouth. "I'm sorry! I can't believe I just did that!"

Stanley laughed. "I'd be disappointed if you didn't! I take that's a yes?"

This time, Callie threw her arms around Sunny's

neck. "Yes. Oh, yes!"

They reached Barn 6 and led Sunny inside. The familiar smells enveloped them—hay and leather, liniment and sweet grain. Home.

Back in the barn, Stanley and Callie went about removing Sunny's harness and washing her down. But Callie had more questions.

"Have you heard anything about Morrison?"

"Fifteen years for blackmail and obstruction of justice. Would have been much different if he had cooperated from the start." Stanley snorted. "Fool thought he was being clever, holding onto that surveillance footage."

As Stanley began rubbing down Sunny, Callie heard footsteps behind her. She turned to find Sarah Ferguson approaching, her designer boots clicking against the concrete aisle.

"Haylie, I mean *Callie*, dear." Ferguson's smile was warm but carried an edge of nervousness. "Might I have a word?"

Callie exchanged a glance with Stanley, who tactfully busied himself with Sunny's leg wraps.

Ferguson led her a few stalls away, out of earshot. "I wanted to thank you."

"Thank me?" Callie's eyebrows rose.

"For your discretion." Ferguson's voice dropped to nearly a whisper. "About what you found in my tack room."

There it was. The conversation they'd never had. The conversation Callie had been dreading and anticipating in equal measure.

"Mrs. Ferguson—"

"Please, let me finish." Ferguson held up one manicured hand. "I was terrified you'd report me to the racing commission. Instead, you said nothing."

Callie chose her words carefully. "I was investigating a fire, not drug violations."

"Still." Ferguson's eyes glistened. "After you left that day, I threw everything away. Every vial, every container. I've been racing and training clean ever since." She paused, her voice cracking slightly. "I was so afraid of losing—of not being competitive—that I was willing to cheat. Willing to risk my horses' health." She shook her head. "The shame of that keeps me awake at night."

"Why are you telling me this?"

"Because I want you to know that sometimes people can change. Sometimes getting caught—or almost getting caught—is exactly what someone needs to finally do the right thing." Ferguson reached out and squeezed Callie's hand. "Thank you for giving me that chance."

She turned and walked away before Callie could respond, her footsteps fading down the aisle.

Stanley had finished with Sunny and was putting away the harness. "What was that about?"

"Second chances," Callie said quietly.

That evening, Callie met Paul at their usual table by the window in the Italian restaurant. The garlic knots were already waiting, the aroma of garlic rising from the basket.

Paul stood as she approached, and the smile that spread across his face—the one that crinkled the corners of his blue eyes—made her heart do that familiar flip it had been doing for months now.

"You're late," he said, pulling out her chair.

"Sunny had her best time yet. Stanley and I were celebrating."

"That calls for more garlic knots." Paul signaled the waitress, who arrived with another basket of steaming hot rolls.

After they'd ordered—chicken parmesan for him,

cheese tortellini with alfredo for her—Paul reached across the table and took her hand.

"I have news," he said.

"Good or bad?"

"Good news. The paper is submitting my articles about Tommy Valdez and the fire at the track for a Pulitzer."

Callie grabbed his hand. "Oh Paul. That's wonderful news. Maybe something good will come of all this after all."

The waitress arrived with their meals, forcing them to separate hands. Callie stared at her tortellini.

Paul set down his fork, his expression growing serious. "Callie, I think something good already has."

Callie looked up. "What?"

"Our partnership."

"Oh." Callie blushed.

"But I've been hoping we could form a new kind of partnership. A permanent one. The kind where we stop writing our stories separately and start writing one together." His cheeks flushed slightly. "The kind where we figure out this whole relationship thing properly instead of dancing around it."

"Paul—"

"I know it's fast." He held up a hand. "I know we've only known each other ten months. But these have been the most intense ten months of my life, and the only thing I'm certain of is that I don't want to do any more of my life without you."

Callie felt tears prick her eyes. She reached for a garlic knot, tore it in half, and passed him half. Their fingers touched as he took it.

"I'll think about it," she said, a smile tugging at her lips.

"That's all I'm asking." He took a bite of the garlic knot.

They ate in comfortable silence for a few minutes before Paul spoke again. "I stopped by to see Marcus Brennan last week."

Callie looked up sharply. "How is he?"

"Better than you'd expect. Worse than he deserves." Paul set down his fork. "He's sold the house. Too many memories, he said. He's moving to Tennessee to be closer to his parents."

"Is he getting out of harness racing?"

"For now. Maybe forever." Paul wiped his mouth with his napkin. "He told me something interesting, though. He had an insurance policy on Thunder's Echo. The insurance company paid out on the horse. The full policy amount—$250,000."

"That's surprising considering..."

"Apparently his was the only name on the policy and he had nothing to do with the fire. So they paid up. What's more, he's donating it all. Every penny. To an equine rescue organization that rehabilitates retired racers." Paul's voice carried a note of admiration. "Said it was blood money and he didn't want any part of it."

Callie felt her throat tighten. Marcus Brennan had lost everything—his horse, his wife, nearly his marriage to the sport he loved. And yet he'd found a way to turn that tragedy into something meaningful.

"There's more," Paul continued. "He asked me to tell you something."

"What's that?"

"He said to tell you that Sunny's recovery gave him hope. That if a horse could heal from the trauma she went through, maybe he could too."

Callie blinked back tears. She reached for her water glass, taking a long sip to steady herself.

"I'm glad he's doing okay," she finally managed.

"He also said he'd be watching Sunny's race in two weeks. He'll be rooting for her."

Two weeks later, Callie sat in the sulky behind Sunny in the paddock for the Meadow Vale Stakes. Eight other fillies and their drivers surrounded her, each preparing in their own way—some talking quietly to their horses, others checking and rechecking their equipment.

Stanley stood at Sunny's head, one hand on her face right between her large, brown eyes. "You remember what I told you?"

"Stay patient. Wait for the seam. Thread the needle."

"And?"

"Racing's won in the stretch, not the first turn."

Stanley grinned. "That's my girl." He stepped back as the marshal signaled it was time to move to the track.

Callie guided Sunny onto the racing surface, and the roar of the crowd washed over them. The grandstand was packed—it was a beautiful spring Saturday, perfect weather for racing. Somewhere in those stands, Paul was watching. Stanley would be at the rail. And maybe, just maybe, Marcus Brennan was watching from Tennessee, rooting for the filly who'd survived her own trauma.

The mobile starting gate rolled into position. Sunny fell into line—post position four this time, a much better draw. Callie felt the familiar flutter of nervous energy mixed with excitement.

The gate picked up speed. Twenty miles per hour. Twenty-five.

At twenty-seven miles per hour, the metal arms swung forward and the truck sped off.

The race began.

Sunny burst forward with power and confidence, finding her stride immediately. No hesitation. No fear. Callie guided her toward the rail, finding an opening as they approached the first turn. They tucked into third place, right where they wanted to be.

Around the first turn. Down the backstretch. Sunny's

breathing was steady, rhythmic. Callie could feel the filly's strength, coiled and ready.

Approaching the far turn, the horse in second position began to fade. The seam appeared, that small opening just big enough to pass through.

Now.

Callie tapped the shaft with her whip. Sunny responded instantly, surging forward, threading through the narrow gap. They moved into second place, then pulled alongside the leader—a gray filly who'd been setting a blistering pace.

Into the final turn. The gray filly was tiring, her stride shortening. Sunny pulled ahead by a length. Then two.

They straightened into the homestretch, and Callie let Sunny have her head. The filly stretched out, eating up ground with every powerful stride. The gray filly tried to rally, but Sunny was too strong, too determined.

They flashed across the finish line three lengths ahead.

The crowd erupted.

Callie eased back on the lines, letting Sunny slow gradually. Her own heart was hammering, tears streaming down her face. They'd done it. After everything—the fire, the investigation, the accident, the long months of rehabilitation—they'd won.

Stanley was waiting at the gap, his face split by the widest grin Callie had ever seen. Behind him, Paul was running across the infield, his notepad forgotten in his pocket, his only focus on reaching her.

As Callie climbed down from the sulky, Paul swept her into his arms, spinning her around while the crowd cheered and cameras flashed.

"I'm so proud of you," he whispered in her ear.

"We did it," Callie said, pulling back to look at Sunny. "She did it."

Stanley was already leading the filly toward the

winner's circle, where a track official waited with a bouquet of roses and a silver trophy that caught the afternoon sun.

As they posed for photos—Callie holding Sunny's lead rope, Stanley beaming beside them, Paul snapping pictures on his phone—Callie felt something settle deep in her chest. Not just satisfaction or pride, though she felt those too.

Peace.

The investigation was over. Tommy Valdez and Frank Morrison would face justice. The insurance claims had been settled. The track had installed new fire suppression systems in every barn and upgraded their security cameras. Life at Liberty Racetrack was moving forward.

And so was she.

That evening, after the celebration had wound down and the crowds had dispersed, Callie found herself back in Barn 6. Sunny was contentedly munching hay in her stall, her winner's blanket draped over her door. Callie leaned against the stall, breathing in the familiar scents of horse and barn.

Paul appeared beside her, two cans of soda in his hands. He passed her one.

"To Sunny," he said, raising his can.

"To Sunny," Callie echoed, clinking her can against his.

They stood in comfortable silence for a moment, watching the filly.

"So," Paul said eventually. "Have you thought about it?"

"Thought about what?" Callie asked, though she knew exactly what he meant.

"My proposal. The partnership. Getting married."

Callie took a sip of ginger ale, letting the moment stretch. Then she turned to face him, a smile playing at her lips.

"I have."

"And?"

"And I think Haylie Norr would have said it was too fast, too risky, too much of an unknown variable."

Paul's face fell slightly.

"But Callie Oaks," she continued, stepping closer to him, "Callie Oaks thinks it sounds perfect."

The smile that spread across Paul's face rivaled the one he'd worn when Sunny crossed the finish line. He set down his soda and pulled her close, his kiss tasting of promise.

In her stall, Sunny nickered softly, as if offering her approval.

Outside, the spring evening settled over Liberty Racetrack. In three months, the track would mark the first anniversary of the fire that had claimed twenty-eight horses and nearly destroyed the tight-knit community that called this place home. But they had survived. They had healed. And they would continue racing forward, one stride at a time.

Because that's what horsemen do. That's what survivors do.

They get back in the sulky, gather the lines, and race toward whatever finish line waited ahead.

And this time, Callie wouldn't be racing alone.

ASHVILLE GAZETTE - SOCIETY

LOCAL JOURNALIST AND SULKY DRIVER ANNOUNCE ENGAGEMENT
By Cindy Grenz

ASHVILLE, PA - Ashville Gazette reporter Paul Coffman popped the question to harness racing driver, Callie Oaks, and she said "Yes."

The couple first met while investigating the fire at Liberty Racetrack nearly a year ago. And sparks began to fly.

"She's the best story I ever covered," Coffman said with a grin.

A summer wedding is planned…

ABOUT THE AUTHOR

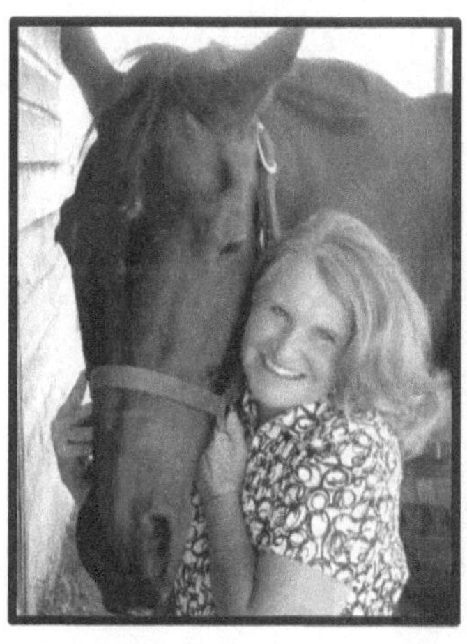

M.J. Evans is the award-winning author of twenty-six published works spanning middle-grade, young adult, and adult fiction, as well as a selection of picture books. Her writing often explores themes centered around horses and equine fantasy, reflecting a lifelong passion for these remarkable animals. A graduate of Oregon State University and a former educator with experience teaching both middle and high school students, Ms. Evans brings both educational insight and storytelling flair to her work. She resides in beautiful Colorado with her husband, Tom, where they enjoy the company of their horses and Standard

Poodle. She is the proud mother of five and grandmother of thirteen.

M.J. Evans was the recipient of the 2024 Colorado Authors League Lifetime Achievement Award.

Literary awards include:
Chanticleer International Book Awards
Readers' Favorite International Awards
Eric Hoffer Awards
Nautilus Awards
Literary Classics awards
Literary Global Book Awards
Feathered Quill Book Awards
Purple Dragonfly Awards
Royal Dragonfly Awards
Page Turner Award
Next Generation Award
Global Book Awards
CIPA Evvy Book Awards
Pinnacle Book Achievement Awards
Incipere Book Awards
International Impact Book Awards
Maincrest Media Book Awards
Book Excellence Awards
Mom's Choice Awards

Visit her website to learn more about the author and her books:

If you enjoyed this book, please take a minute to post a short review on Amazon. That helps others find the book as well.

You can contact M.J. Evans on her website: **www.dancinghorsepress.com.** She loves to receive letters, and she always writes back!

Follow her on social media:
Goodreads:
https://www.goodreads.com/author/show/4496514.M J Evans
Bookbub:
https://www.bookbub.com/profile/m-j-evans

Amazon:
https://www.amazon.com/stores/M.-J.-Evans/author/B004GMS014
Instagram:
https://www.instagram.com/mjevansbooks
Facebook:
https://www.facebook.com/profile.php?id=615535 22941532

Join her email list for occasional updates on new releases and receive a FREE PDF of a short Christmas story. Email her at **mjevansbtm@gmail.com** and put "Join email list" in the subject line

Read more Award-Winning Titles by M.J. Evans:

Novels:
Fire at the Track
Coal Dust and Dreams
Finding Fionn
The Stallion and His Peculiar Boy
In the Heart of a Mustang
The Sand Pounder
PINTO!
North Mystic
Mr. Figgletoes' Toy Emporium

Biography:
Silver Charm

Fantasy Series:
The Mist Trilogy-
Behind the Mist
Mists of Darkness
The Rising Mist

The Centaur Chronicles-
The Stone of Mercy
The Stone of Courage
The Stone of Integrity
The Stone of Wisdom

Picture Books:
Percy-The Racehorse Who Didn't Like to Run
The Skullington Family Series-
Boney Fingers
Bone Appetit
School is a Grave Mistake
Skeletons in the Closet

Equestrian Trail Guidebooks for Colorado
Riding Colorado
Riding Colorado II
Riding Colorado III
Riding Colorado and Beyond

All titles are available on the website:
www.dancinghorsepress.com
And wherever books are sold.

Acknowledgements

I am so grateful to the people who have helped me with this book. Growing up in Pony Club, I knew a lot about horses in general, and jumping and dressage in particular. But I am not an expert in harness racing. So, I called on a few people who are!

My thanks go to:

Cheryl Eriksen, the author of *Greyhound—The Remarkable Story of the Legendary Racehorse Who Inspired a Nation.*

Ashley Dailey, a third-generation harness horseman, whose family trains full-time. Her father was inducted into the Ohio Hall of Fame for his success as a trainer. Ashley works for the Ohio Harness Horsemen's Association as an on-air commentator and contributes to their publications.

And to Richard G. Stone who has spent his entire career in the harness racing world. He spent decades as the yearling manager for Castleton Farm in Lexington, Kentucky.

Of course, no book would be worth reading without the careful evaluation and corrections provided by an editor. I am so grateful for my editor, Denny Dressman. Denny is the author of numerous books, including the just-released book, "Black Baseball's Heyday: Capturing an Era in Art and Words." After a quarter of a century, Denny retired from his job as a sports editor for the Rocky Mountain News in Denver and is now writing and editing.